The Cactus Valley Boarding School

The Cactus Valley Boarding School

Sandra Joy

iUniverse, Inc.
Bloomington

The Cactus Valley Boarding School

iUniverse books may be ordered through booksellers or by contacting:

iUniverse
1663 Liberty Drive
Bloomington, IN 47403
www.iuniverse.com
1-800-Authors (1-800-288-4677)

ISBN: 978-1-4620-2689-0 (sc)
ISBN: 978-1-4620-2690-6 (ebk)

Printed in the United States of America

iUniverse rev. date: 06/27/2011

TABLE OF CONTENTS

INTRODUCTORY

KATE couldn't believe it! She had just found out her parents and those of her three best friends, Helen Stacy, Miley Johnson, and Annie Randolf, had decided to send them to boarding school for their senior year of high school. How could her own parents do this to her? Her parents knew she didn't like jumping into big things like this without a *lot* of serious consideration. She had never been away from home for longer than the weekend, and then never out of the country without her parents, so why were they doing this to her? She didn't know anyone there, so the only people she'd know would be Helen, Annie, and Miley. No, they weren't exactly popular at the public school they had been attending for the past few years, but at least they were used to the way things were. And she'd have to live there for an entire school year! Were her parents out of their minds?

Kate's parents were not out of their mind. They were simply sending her there because they thought it was time Kate learned to live her life without depending on them all the time. Since she was 17, they wanted her to become more independent. Another reason they were sending her away was because both parents had a job. Her father was a trucker, and therefore barely ever home. Her mother was a newspaper editor for the local paper. She had recently gotten a promotion. Before she had received the promotion, she had always been home in time to get supper, but after the promotion, she wasn't home until around 8 or 9 o'clock. And besides, the challenge would be good for her. Of course, they were a little worried of how she'd do being miles away, but they didn't let her know that.

Kate's friends actually kind of liked the idea. Of course, they didn't like leaving their friends behind, and they were a little nervous. But they were also a little excited at the challenge. So they tried to get Kate cheered up and excited as well.

"Come on, Kate, what are you worried about? It'll be fun."

"We'll get to meet all these hot guys and go shopping together."

"We'll even be able to live together!"

Her friends soon cheered her up and by the time they were on their way, Kate was almost excited as the others. Though she was still somewhat frightened, she was no longer angry at her parents. She didn't embrace the idea entirely yet, but it did have its good points. She knew that with her friends there with her, she'd be alright.

CHAPTER ONE

ARRIVAL

They had finally reached their destination, The Cactus Valley Boarding School Of Dallas, Texas. It was just after 1 o'clock on Monday. Kathlyn Farrell, Annie Randolph, Helen Stacy, and Miley Johnson were somewhat scared, anxious and nervous as they arrived at the Cactus Valley Boarding School in the taxi that had brought them from the airport.

'I'm sure there had to be another Boarding School in Minnesota where we could attend,' Kate thought wryly, though she was really starting to like the idea of living in Texas for about a year. She hadn't exactly jumped at the idea of going to the Boarding School at first. But, the more she thought about it, the more she liked it. It would give her a chance to get away and experience something new, different for a change. Not all changes are a bad thing, right? Kate sure hoped so. And the more she thought about it, the more she liked the idea of being hundreds of miles away from her everyday life.

They all climbed out of the taxi. Picking up their suitcases, they looked around. The building was a huge reddish/brown brick building. It was a dormitory as well as the school all in one big building with the school in the middle of the guys' and the girls' dorms. The words, Cactus Valley Boarding School, were written in big bold, black letters above the double doors of the building. They climbed up the front steps and through the large, brown, double doors. Just inside was a beautiful lobby. It was carpeted in dark green and had medium green walls. There was one set of stairs on either side of a long hallway at the far wall. Above each doorway of the staircases was a sign. The sign above the doorway on the left said 'men' and the one on the right said 'ladies'. On either side the entrance doors and along the left wall was what looked like a waiting area with couches strewn along side the wall. On the right wall was a closed door marked 'Office'. Even though it was two days till school started students were everywhere. Some were whispering excitedly, others not so quietly and the new comers were hardly noticed as they entered.

Before Kate and her friends could decide whether to knock on the door or not, it opened, and a somewhat pretty, middle aged woman came out. She was of average height and slender. Her mouth was set in a thin serious line, which made her look somewhat mean. But when she saw them, she smiled, and her face became instantly friendlier. "You must be the girls from Minnesota. We've been expecting you. My name is Mrs. Mueller. I'm your principal. Why don't you follow me into my office and we can sign all the necessary papers. Then I'll show you to your rooms." Mrs. Mueller's office was astounding. It didn't even look like an office. Well, it did, a little. There was a desk built close to the wall at the far end of the room with a chair standing behind it. Filing cabinets were built into the right wall. In the front off the room was a sitting area made up of some couches, chairs, a coffee table in the middle and a TV set in front of it. The floor was covered in a beautiful dark red carpet and the walls were painted in swirls with pail pinkish-red paint.

Once all the papers was taken care of, she showed them to their rooms in the ladies' dorm. At the top of the staircase, the hallway made a sharp right turn. A long straight hallway with doors on either side met the girl's curious stare.

"The first 2 rooms are yours," the principal said. "One on either side. There will be two girls in each room, and you may choose your own roommates. The numbers to the combination locks are in the rooms on your dressers. You are expected to remember them. In case you forget them we also have them recorded in our office. But you should be responsible enough to remember them. Take the next hour to get settled in and unpacked. Then in an hour come meet me in the lobby and I'll give you a tour of the place and we'll figure out your class schedules. We'll also go over the rules you'll be expected to follow. Don't be late." The last sentence was given quite firmly and the girls knew she meant business. She smiled and hurried back down the stairs. The girls raised their eyebrows at each other and grinned. Annie, who loved to tease more then anyone else, put on a straight face and mimicked Mrs. Mueller exactly, "Don't be late." Laughing, they chose their partners.

In ten minutes everyone had been paired off into groups of two and were in their rooms unpacking. Kate and Miley paired off while Helen and Annie shared the room right across from them. Miley's and Kate's room number was 102 and Helen's and Annie's room number was 101. The room was not very big but not crowded either. There were two windows that looked out unto the large lawn. Under the left window stood a small night stand. On either side of the stand was a single bed. Along the front wall stood two large dressers, on one of which was a piece of paper which read '17-357-16'. Miley figured it out first. "I guess this is our lock code. Better not lose it." On either side of the room stood a desk with a chair beside a closet.

"Wow," Kate breathed, "I can't believe I'm really and truly here. I keep pinching myself to make sure I'm not dreaming," Kate laughed. Miley laughed, too.

"It is amazing, isn't it?" They unpacked as quickly as possible while they talked. "I'm so glad my parents let me come."

"Me, too. I just hope we'll be able to get a job somewhere around close by. Wouldn't it be neat if we could work together in the same place?" Kate was, as usual, jumping ahead of herself, but in the excitement of being in Dallas, one could say its quite normal.

"It'd be awesome. But lets worry about that later. Right now we better wash up and go downstairs or we'll be late. Remember? 'don't be late'," she said. Her imitation was almost as perfect as Annie's had been. They both burst out laughing, and hurried to wash up. They reached the hallway at the same time as Helen and Annie.

They got a tour of the building, but it wasn't the principal that showed them around, it was a somewhat irritated teacher. One that hardly looked older than any of the girls themselves. Her name was Miss Rockheart. She was about an inch or two taller then Kate which meant she had to be round 5ft. and 7 inches to 5ft. 8 inches. It seemed she would much rather do something more fun then show the girls around, but she was particularly nice to the guys that passed. They learned where the Library, the nurse's office, classrooms, washrooms, gym, swimming pools; an outdoor one and an indoor one; as well as the laundry room, were located. They also met the Librarian, Mrs. Wilder. They were told they could meet the other teachers later. Kate's favourite places were the swimming pools and the library.

* * *

They had just received their schedules and finished their tour. Now it was time to go to the first class of the school year. The class was to go over the rules for the school and laws of Dallas, Texas. Everyone had to attend this class and she and her friends were scheduled to attend the 4 o'clock class. Kate, Miley, Helen, and Annie entered the class. It was still 5 minutes to four but it seemed everyone was accounted for. In the front of the room stood two young, good looking men and a pretty brunette who was short, slender and very tanned. The men were also very tanned, and both muscular and tall, one had brown hair while the other had blond hair.

"I've seen tons of hott guys, but these two beat them all," Helen whispered. "I mean, look at those muscle."

"Stop drooling," Miley teased. But Annie, Miley and Kate couldn't help but agree. They looked around. There were guys and girls standing in small clusters here and there. Especially toward the front of the class. Kate noticed the two hott guys in the front of the room were not the only hott guys in the room. Not that it mattered, of course. Another thing she had noticed was that almost everyone in Texas that she had seen so far was tanned. Very beautifully tanned.

"Why don't we sit in the front?" Annie suggested. Kate grinned and shook her head. "Two reasons," she said, "One, the front seats are all taken, and two, we didn't come here to gape at the teachers." Annie and Helen were the biggest flirts she knew and the guys back home knew it too. The guys around here would probably find out very fast. The girls all laughed. Grinning, then took seats towards the back of the class. Just as they sat down, Mrs. Mueller entered the classroom. She walked to the front of the class and everybody that wasn't already sitting, took a seat. She waited till the room was quiet before speaking.

"Good afternoon, everyone, first of all I'd like to introduce you to my friends, Annette Shirley and Dwayne Curtiss. They are part of the police force. They will help you get more familiar with the laws of Dallas. Andrew Urban here is one of our handymen. You'll probably meet the other two pretty soon." Their names even suited them, Kate thought. The one with the brown hair was Dwayne, and the blond haired one was Andrew. She found the laws to be very much the same as those of Minnesota's, so she listened only half-heartedly. When they had finished with the laws and warnings of Dallas, Mrs. Mueller told them the rules of the school.

The girls learned that on weekdays, as of Sundays through Thursdays, their curfew was at 10:30 p.m. and on Fridays and Saturdays, it was at 11:30 p.m. Lights out was at 10:45 p.m. sharp on weekdays and at 11:45 p.m. sharp on weekends. One rule the girls had been informed of before leaving Minnesota was the no cell phone rule. That was also the only rule that Kate, Annie, Miley, and Helen had no intention of obeying. They had decided to keep their phones on themselves and hidden at all times just in case somebody decided to search their rooms while they weren't in it. They had been warned that they weren't to hide things in their room that were against the rules just in case somebody searched their rooms, which was likely to happen. Other then that they had decided to behave and obey the rest of the rules if at all possible.

CHAPTER TWO

FITTING IN AND TROUBLE

They had a job!! Kate and Miley got a job in a casual restaurant called Arbys, while Annie and Helen got a job in a clothing store called Kelly's Clothing just one block away. They were both in the same direction so they would walk, or run when they were late, to work together. Since Arbys was open later then Kelly's, Helen and Annie would often come there after work if they didn't have too much homework and wait for them so that they could go home together. It seems that the only time all four of them could have some private time together was on their way to and from work. But that, too, changed as they made new friends.

Two weeks had gone by. Kate and her friends were doing well with their studies. And they had made a few new friends. First Helen, who was by far the most outgoing of the foursome, met Rachael. Rachael's favourite subject was guys. She was a total flirt just like Annie and Helen and so the three fit together splendidly. Then Annie had met Jannette, when Jannette was shopping at Kelly's during Annie's shift. Jane, as everyone called her, also attended the Boarding School and worked part time at a hair salon as a hair stylist. So, she was also very busy and they didn't see each other much outside of school, but she did teach them some pretty cool hairdos. Miley, Helen and Annie had also met the other two handymen. One was Steve Parker and the other was Cori Conroy. Though Kate had not as yet been introduced to Steve, she had met Cori.

They had also gotten a few enemies. Their number one enemy was Miranda, or better known as Randi, and then came her friends, Lori, and Melissa. They always did everything possible to make life as miserable as they could for Kate and her friends. Miranda especially seemed to have it in for Kate.

They were busy but happy. Well, most of the time. There were times when Kate, and Miley, who loved to write, or rather type, would much rather be writing a story then studying. Annie and Helen didn't much like to write or type so they would rather go for a swim then write. And they missed their families and other friends back home. Thankfully, they had Sundays entirely to themselves which they usually spent going to church, studying, calling home, relaxing, swimming, writing or reading, and shopping.

There was also the fact the someone was trying to get Kate in trouble, or so it seemed anyway. Lately, one of the many beautiful trophies that stood proudly in the Trophy Case in the Lobby had disappeared. Annette and Dwayne had been trying to find the thief and the trophy ever since it disappeared, but it was Randi who found it three days after it was discovered missing when she 'accidentally' opened Kate's locker and found it standing on the shelf. Randi had said she had thought it was her own locker and that's why she had opened it. Randi had developed a strong dislike towards Kate almost upon meeting her and therefore Kate didn't really believe Randi had accidentally thought that it was her own locker, for Randi's locker was all the way down the hall. Kate figured Randi had known it was there and had opened her locker on purpose. But how the trophy had gotten there, she had no idea. And how had Randi known it was there?

Kate hadn't even known what the trophy looked like that had gone missing, (she wasn't one to pay much attention to those kind of things) and told Mrs. Mueller, Annette, and Dwayne, who were interrogating her, exactly that. She certainly hadn't put it in her locker. She didn't even know what use a trophy would be to her and therefore had no reason to steal one. And there was no way she would be crazy enough to steal a trophy only to hide it in her very own locker. She reasoned with them, "If I had stolen it, which I definitely didn't, I would have taken it as far away from here as possible. Someplace you guys wouldn't think to look for it. But like I said, I didn't do it and I don't plan on stealing in the future either. Somebody must have put it there to frame me." And as if to prove her point she added, "I once stole a quarter from a school cupcake sale when I was a kid and I still feel guilty about it." That made them smile, but she could tell they weren't entirely convinced.

"Do you have any idea of who would want to frame you?" Annette asked. Kate had a feeling she did. But she wasn't going to tell them just yet and maybe never. So she just shook her head.

"I guess its a good thing its back safely, unhurt. We'll forget about it and just hope none other disappear." They had let her go then. Kate decided to forget it, but only for now. She would worry 'bout it later. And hope that it was the first and last trophy to disappear. The first and last anything to disappear for that matter.

* * *

Kate ran down the hall to her room. Oh, she knew she shouldn't be running, she had gotten in trouble more then once already for running in the hall, but she was late for work already as it was. She should've been at work for the past five minutes and she still had to change and do her hair before getting to work. Rhonda Santiago, her boss, was very strict about appearances. Though Rhonda was usually easy to please, she wouldn't tolerate her employees being late or messy and certainly not both. Rhonda was sure to be angry today. Not that Kate blamed her.

'Why do I always get myself in trouble? Why didn't I go with Miley when she asked me to? Then at least I wouldn't be late. Why do I always read till the very last minute? Why do I love to read so much?' She fumed. She was angry at herself and therefore yelling at herself, not that it was doing any good. The fact that she could get lost in any good book and even forget the time and where she was, had often gotten her in trouble in the past and she was sure it would do so in the future as well, just as it had now.

* * *

He punched in the lock code number Mrs. Mueller had given him and entered room 102. He had been assured that the occupants of the room were both at work at this time of day and therefore they had decided that Cori didn't need to stand watch, for it would just arise the suspicion of those that happened to pass the room. Once inside the room, Steve was amazed at the looks of it. There were pictures and posters all over the four walls, one could barely make out the color of the wall. Shaking his head, he smiled. The pictures must be of their friends and family in Minnesota. But he had no time to muse and check them all out, he had work to do. Just as he was about to open the top drawer of the nightstand between the beds, the door opened and someone entered the room.

CHAPTER THREE

CAUGHT

Steve spun around to face the intruder. Only it wasn't really an intruder. It was Kathlyn, or better known as Kate. He recognized her immediately as Miley's roommate. He had never met her but he had seen her before and could recognize her upon sight. But what was she doing here? She was supposed to be at work. But there was no time to ponder and think about it. He needed an excuse. She had turned pale when she saw him. He opened his mouth to speak, but she beat him to it.

"What the . . . ?! Who are you? What are you doing in here?" But she didn't give him a chance to speak. "Never mind! Forget it! I'm late and I don't have time to talk. Just get out of here! I need to get changed and get to work! Or my boss will have my head. Now go!! Get out!! You can come back in here once I'm done and look for whatever you were looking for." And with that she pushed him out of the room and slammed the door.

Wow! What a girl! Was he lucky or what? Hopefully she had been so busy telling him to get out, she wouldn't have seen his face enough to recognize him if she saw him again. But no, he knew better than that. He knew she had seen him and would most likely recognize him. Well, he had better not be standing in the hall when she came back or she would most definitely know he had been looking for something. But how had she known he was looking for something? Or had she just figured that that's what a handyman would want in her room? Something wasn't right. Well, he better warn Mrs. Mueller. Why had he agreed to do that anyway? He was so busy thinking that he didn't even see her running past him on his way down the staircase.

* * *

"So what do I do now?" Steve asked.

"Well, we have to find out if she'd recognize you if she saw you again." Mrs. Mueller said thoughtfully. "Kate works at Arbys, so why don't you take a friend or two and grab a bite to eat there? She's bound to see you and I'm sure she'll say something if she recognizes you."

Steve didn't like this awkward situation, but he agreed to do it. "And what if she does recognize me?" He asked. "What am I supposed to do? Tell her that she was right? That I was looking for something?" He groaned. The fact that her guess had been right was scary.

"I'm sure you'll think of something," Mrs. Mueller smiled. "But no, don't tell her that. We want her to trust us and she's not the kind of person who'll easily trust someone. You've got to work to earn her trust. If she thinks we're suspecting her, she won't trust us and then she'll definitely not help us."

"Why do you think she doesn't trust people easily?" Steve was interested. This sounded unlike any young girl he'd ever met.

* * *

An hour later, Steve, Cori, and Andrew were seated in a booth at Arbys by Miley. Andrew shot Steve a look that said, "This her?" Steve shook his head. Cori, who had met Miley, always loved a good conversation, especially with a girl, and Miley was no different. He loved talking to her.

"Hello, Miley. Didn't expect to see you here." He grinned.

She grinned back at him, "Yeah right. You knew perfectly well that I work here."

"Ok, ok. You got me. You see, you're so charming I just couldn't stay away."

"No, you're not supposed to come to Arby's because of the waitresses, you're supposed to come because of the food." Miley laughed.

"Well, I come for a little of both." Cori grinned. "Why weren't you at the birthday party last night?"

Miley shrugged, "I was too busy."

"Don't you ever have time to hang out with friends?" Cori frowned.

"Yes, of course. But usually not for parties and things like that. I wanna keep up with my studies, you know." Miley smiled.

"What time do you finish with work?"

"Anywhere between 9 to 9:30." She narrowed her eyes, smiling in a flirtatious manner, "What do you have in mind?"

Just then Kate walked up to the table. She recognized the guys to be the three handymen at the Boarding School though she had only actually met Cori and Andrew. She grinned at Miley, and shook her head in mock disdain, "Miley, girl! You're supposed to serve these poor guys food! Here," she held out a couple of menus. "I just saw Rhonda enter the Restaurant," she winked.

"Oh, did I forget to mention I also have a very annoying friend who is always on my back to get me to work instead of have fun." Miley made a face, addressing the guys. "But its a good thing too, or else I'd probably fail at least half of my subjects, and lose this job." Then she turned her attention to Kate, "Thanks, you always manage to save my back, don't you?!" Miley smiled, taking the menus. Then she got a mischievous twinkle in her eye. "But did you have to interrupt? We were in the middle of a very interesting conversation."

"So I heard," Kate said grinning. "I'll leave you alone now. Just wish me luck on saving my own back." Kate rolled her eyes, "I still have to tell her I was late today." Sending the guys a smile, glancing at the darker one, the one she hadn't met yet, again, whom, she knew she had seen lately, but she couldn't quite place yet as to where, or why she all of a sudden had a suspicious feeling about him, then she turned around and headed after Rhonda, who had just entered the kitchen.

Kate had told Miley about the intruder as soon as she had gotten to Arbys. As well as why she was late. She was determined to not only find out who this guy was, but also the reason as to why he had been in their room in the first place. But she had a pretty good guess as to what he had been looking for; the trophy that had disappeared only the day before. This was the second trophy that had disappeared this year. It worried her. She hoped this one wouldn't also appear among her things like the other one had. But right now she had to focus on not getting fired. And after that, she'd spend a little more time looking for the thief. "Rhonda, I need to talk to you."

"Fire away." Rhonda replied.

Kate didn't like beating 'round the bush so she got right down to the point, "I got to work 20 minutes late today."

"Why is that?"

"Weeell, to make a long story short, I was reading in my History text book, lost track of time, and ended up being late. I'm sorry." After a short lecture on punctuality, she was ordered back to work with a friendly shove.

"Here, bud, can you take this plate and follow me?" It was Miley.

"Sure thing. Whose order is this?"

Miley looked at her and grinned. Kate raised her eyebrows. "The guys'?!" Miley nodded. They both laughed as they headed toward the guys.

"Here ya go," Miley grinned her million dollar grin. Kate studied the dark haired guy. Was this the guy that had been in her room earlier? Or was it just another guy that looked just like him? He seemed somewhat nervous under her gaze. Or was that just her imagination? She decided she had nothing to lose so why not ask him.

"So did you find what you were looking for earlier on?" She asked with a soft teasing smile on her lips.

He hesitated. He was caught for sure now. He had gotten uneasy as she studied him and he knew she was wondering whether or not he was the guy in her room this afternoon, and he was sure when she asked him that question. Yet he had to try and look innocent. "What do ya mean?" Darn it! His hesitation had given him away. He could tell by the look in her eye.

"Why don't you tell me?" She turned to Miley, "You better get back to work before we both get in trouble. You know how Rhonda hates it when there's two waitresses at the same table. And, I have a little something I wanna talk to the guys about." Kate flashed Miley a grin. "I'll tell you all about it later. And you can have the guys back as soon as I'm done."

The guys noticed both girls had very similar, beautiful smiles. But they also noticed that they saw Miley's smile a whole lot more often then Kate's. Kate's smile was forced more often then not. Her brilliant one was usually hiding. She always seemed to be troubled about something.

Miley feigned a pout, "Spoilsport!" Then she smiled, "Alright, I'll go but I wanna hear every single word of it later on. And hurry up." She said grinning. She flashed the guys a mischievous grin and a wink. "Later." Then turned and hurried away. Once Miley was gone, Kate once more turned her attention to the guys, and waited.

The guys started explaining that some guy in room 102 in the guys' dorm had asked Cori to fix the window in his room, but Cori had been busy so he had asked Steve to do it for him, but Cori had forgotten to mention whether it was the guys' dorm room or the girls'. And Steve, finding everything ok in the guy's room, figured he had meant the girls' room. And so therefore had gone in there.

Steve finished the explanation with, "I'm sorry I made such a dumb mistake. I can't believe I did that," Then he looked at her expectedly, and almost forgot what he had been saying. The way she stood there, with those flashing dark green eyes, that pointed nose, those naturally red lips made him wish they were in a completely different setting and talking about something else or even saying nothing at all. Somehow he knew she wasn't even wearing make up and yet she looked stunning. But what was that look in her eyes? Annoyance? Impatience? Humour? Anger? All of the above? She was a mystery to him. No girl had ever been a mystery before. He could always figure them out. But this one was different. He couldn't figure her out and he hated it. Then she laughed.

"You actually expect me to believe that? Come on, I know I'm not the brightest person around, but I know you were looking through my room. I was kind of expecting it even before I was warned before I got here that someone might check my room every now and then. Though I can't say as I like that idea very much. I like my privacy, you know? But, I guess you got to do what you got to do, huh?" Kate gave him a wry smile.

He was saved from giving an answer by Rhonda who shot Kate a look that said, 'You had better get back to work, young lady,' as she passed their table. Kate nodded at her, and excused herself.

"Well that answers that question, huh? She does recognize me. And she also knows what I was doing! Now what do I do?" Steve muttered, "What kind of mess have I got myself into? And, I made up that whole stupid story 'bout getting the rooms mixed up. Now she'll think I'm a total jerk."

"Does it matter what she thinks? I mean, she's just another girl, isn't she?" Cori loved teasing him about girls.

CHAPTER FOUR

MORE TROUBLE

"I honestly can't believe I agreed to do this." Kate groaned.

"Oh, come on, there's nothing to worry about. It's not even really a date. It's just a business date." Miley gently reminded. Ever since her social life had been turned upside down by some people back home, who had spread rumour after rumour around about her that hadn't an ounce of truth in it, Kate had turned down every single guy that had asked her out. She had been quite upset when Miley had told her that she had promised Cori that they'd meet Cori, Andrew and Steve at a restaurant called Bridges at seven, 'to talk business' that night. Miley had dated Cori several times already, but Kate didn't really believe that the two of them would actually stay together for long, for Miley never stuck with one guy for very long.

"Yeah, and I have a feeling I know what business that is." Kate muttered. Suddenly her thoughts turned toward the conversation she had accidentally overheard between Lori, Melissa and Randi. It had gone something like this:

"'Randi, I don't like it. It's too-I don't know-crazy!" Lori whined.

"I agree. It's getting out of hand. One of these days we'll get caught." Mel groaned.

"Look, you know we have to do this, right? We all need the money and we certainly will not be working when we could be having fun like those Minnesota girls do. And besides, you know Millard Miller, he'd turn us over to the authorities if we stop now."'

That's when she had heard footsteps and had had to hurry away. This Millard didn't sound like a pleasant person to deal with. Obviously whatever they were doing wasn't good. At first she had been tempted to tell Mrs. Mueller, Annette, and Dwayne, but the way their voices sounded made her stop and think. It had sounded as though they were having an argument. She still hadn't figured out what she was going to do but she knew she couldn't tell anyone else what she had heard, at least not yet. She had to figure out what they were doing first.

"Come on, lighten up, we're all just friends, ok? Are you ready?" Miley tried to cheer up her friend. Miley was wearing a simple yet dazzling dark green dress with short puffed up sleeves and a long skirt with a ruffled hem. Her long dark hair was done up in a messy bun. She looked great.

"A friends date, huh? Then how come you never dress up like that when us friends go out?" Kate couldn't help but tease Miley just a bit. Kate was wearing a dark red blouse and black jeans. She had half of her thick, long, curly, blond hair done up in a high ponytail while the rest was left to fall freely over her shoulders. She, too, looked great.

Miley gave her a friendly shove, "Whatever." They both laughed.

"Yeah, I'm ready. Let's go." Kate forced a smile. So she and Miley started walking toward the restaurant. Kate had flatly refused the guys' offer of giving them a ride. She still wanted as little to do with guys as possible. So they had agreed to meet at the restaurant. Miley and Kate had decided to walk instead of taking a Taxi for two reasons. One was the weather was perfect for taking a walk and the second was that they didn't really have the money to take a taxi.

The guys arrived at the restaurant first. They decided to take a seat and wait inside. They didn't have to wait long, for the girls arrived a few minutes later. Steve immediately noticed Kate hesitated just inside the door. She looked really nervous, and pale.

"I wonder why she's so nervous," Steve wondered out loud.

"Well, Miley once started to tell me something about Kate and guys, but she was immediately quiet, and when I asked her to go on she just said that Kate trusted her to keep it quiet and she didn't wanna betray that trust. I have a feeling she had a pretty dark background back in Minnesota. I'm just kinda wondering if she left it all behind or if she's brought it with her." Cori said.

"I've never seen her go out with a guy here yet," Andrew remarked.

"That's because she hasn't gone out with a guy here." Cori answered.

"You don't think she's *never* gone out with a guy, do you?" Steve asked.

Andrew shrugged, "Wouldn't know."

"No, I asked Miley that same question once and she said that Kate had gone out with more than one guy. I started asking her more about it and she just said if there were things that we wanted to know 'bout Kate, we'd have to ask her." Cori said.

The girls slowly approached the table and sat down. They all exchanged greetings. "Here's your menus," Andrew said sliding two menus towards them.

"Thanks," they said in unison. They both smiled. Everyone quietly looked over their menus.

Kate was the first to speak, "I don't even know what half of this stuff is. Maybe I'll just get something to drink. I'm not hungry anyway."

"No, I think you had better get something solid into your stomach. By the looks of you, you haven't been feeding yourself properly." Andrew noted. The others nodded in agreement.

"I agree, Kate. You don't wanna look like a skeleton at Christmas, do you?" Miley teased gently. Kate rolled her eyes.

"Who made you guys my keepers?" Then she grinned, "Alright, alright, if you all explain to me what all this food is, I'll eat."

When their food arrived, they pretty much ate in silence. Kate and Miley had begun to wonder if there actually was any business that needed to be discussed, when Andrew cleared his throat. "I'm sure you are both aware of the second trophy that went missing." At their nods, he continued, "You wouldn't by any chance have any idea of who might steal a trophy, would you?"

Miley shook her head, "No I don't."

Kate, who was easily suspicious and offended, was angry. He was practically accusing them of being the thieves. How annoying. But then again, she had been accused of things she hadn't done for so long now, she should be used to it. But, how could a person get used to having ones 'friends' accusing one falsely? Did one ever get used to something like that?

Steve watched Kate closely. At first he could see anger and resentment in her eyes, then sadness and bitterness, and as she turned her head to face Andrew, he saw she had masked her eyes so perfectly, he almost wondered if he had only been seeing things that weren't really there. But he could tell by the sound in her voice that he hadn't been making those things up. He wondered why she was like that. What had happened to her, or had she always been this way?

"No. I do not know anything 'bout the stolen trophy. I heard it was stolen, but that's all." She said thinly. When the guys exchanged looks, she said, "Look, if you blame me for the stolen trophy, I understand. After all, the first trophy was found in my locker." All this she spoke with a calmness that she didn't feel. She wished she could scream and shout at them and even hit them. And at the same time she wished she could just curl up and cry. Or even die.

"No, Kate, we are not blaming you for the stolen trophy. We just thought since you are pretty well known and looked up to and all, maybe you could help us out by giving us all the information you have." Andrew assured.

"Well, I have no information 'bout the trophy." Kate still looked upset.

"Alright, let us just forget it and enjoy ourselves for the rest of the evening then."

Just then Kate's phone started buzzing in her pocket. "Excuse me, I'll be right back." She murmured.

She hurried to the ladies room. Once inside a stall, she took her phone out of her pocket. *Missed call. Sandi Reiley. 7:30.* She checked her messages, but there were no new messages. She wondered why Sandi would call without texting her first to make sure it was ok to call like she usually did. Something must be wrong. *'Hey, I'm at a restaurant with Miley rite now and there's some guys wit us so I can't call u back just yet. Is somethin wrong?'* Then she pressed send. She decided to wait till a return message before going back. Thankfully she didn't have to wait long.

'Nothin really, I just need some advice from you rite now, but I wanna tell u the whole thing, not text it to u so call me as soon as u can, k? But don't panic, its nothin very serious.' 'Gotcha, will do as soon as I can.'

She had just stepped out of the stall when Miley entered the ladies room. "Hey, we were starting to worry about you. Is everything alright?"

"Yeah, don't worry. I just got a phone call from Sandi. And don't worry, I didn't answer. I just texted her and she says she needs some advice and I'm supposed to call her as soon as possible." Kate whispered. "Now lets quickly go back before they start thinking that we left without them noticing." So they hurried back to their table. The guys smiled at them as they sat back down.

"Everything alright?"

"Yeah, we're fine."

Steve, who had been watching Kate as closely as possible without her becoming very aware of it, again noticed that her smiled wasn't as bright as Miley's. She looked a little distracted. Though she hadn't been aware of it, he had noticed she had turned a little red before she left. Was she that upset at Andrew for asking them about the trophy? Was she hiding something? Now where had that thought come from? What would this girl have to hide? What about this trophy? Had she taken it? But she was usually honest, wasn't she? And they hadn't found anything in her room the last time they had gone through it. Except, she wasn't honest about her health. His thoughts ran back to the day before at lunch time.

She had been walking as fast as she could without running and as she had rounded a corner she had slammed right into him. Neither had been paying much attention to their surroundings and therefore had run into each other. They were picking up her books and the few books and papers he had been carrying as Mrs. Mueller rounded the corner and asked what had happened. "I was in a hurry, wasn't watching where I was going, and ran into him." Kate had said in a monotonous voice.

"You weren't running again, were you?" Mrs. Mueller had asked.

"Nope, not this time."

"I'm glad you're finally learning to slow down. It's been a week now since the last time you were caught running in the halls, right?"

Kate had sighed, "Ya, since the last time I got caught."

"So you have run again after that. Am I right?" Mrs. Mueller asked sternly.

Kate looked away. She sighed again and nodded. "Yeah. Yeah, I did. This morning. I was almost late for class." She admitted glumly. Mrs. Mueller had started giving her a lecture, but Kate had interrupted her. "Look, I really don't need another lecture right now, ok? I know what you're gonna say and I know you want what's best for me, I understand that, but I only run if that's the only way I'm going to get where I need to go on time. Now I have a load of homework I have to get halfway through during lunch and I really don't want to be late for class again. 'Cuz then I'll have to run again."

Mrs. Mueller had studied her. Kate had been pale and she had dark circles around her eyes. "You're not sick, are you?" Mrs. Mueller had been concerned, but Kate had pushed her concern aside.

"I'm fine. Nothing to worry 'bout. Just a little tired. Now if you'll excuse me, I have to go." And she had rushed on again. Andrew's voice brought him back to the present.

CHAPTER FIVE

GETTING INVOLVED

"I've got to go. I still have some other things to take care of. You guys will be alright without me, right?" Andrew teased.

"Don't worry, we'll take good care of these ladies here." Steve answered Andrew, but he was watching Kate's reaction as he spoke. But Kate's face was expressionless. So Andrew left, which meant there was only Kate, Miley, Steve and Cori left at the restaurant. After a while of chatting, Cori asked Miley to dance.

Miley looked questioningly at Kate for she knew Kate would hate to be alone with Steve. Kate knew how much her friend loved to dance with Cori so she smiled and shrugged as if to say 'don't worry 'bout me.' Miley flashed her a relieved smile and let Cori lead her to the dance floor. Kate watched them for a while. She could feel Steve's eyes on her. She just hoped with all her heart he wouldn't asked her to dance because she knew she'd have to turn the invitation down. She flashed Steve a smile but turned her attention elsewhere again and was soon lost in thought.

She was worried about Sandi. What kind of advice did she need? If only she could call her. Just then she saw a payphone on the wall close to the entrance. How had she not noticed it before? Could she? Should she? Did she dare? She glanced at Steve. He was still watching her. Should she ask him? She would. She glanced at him again and decided it was now or never.

"W-Would you, uh, mind if I used the pay phone to call one of my friends back home? She's been wanting me to call her for a while now and I just haven't gotten to it yet. I never seem to find the time. Is it alright?"

She hadn't looked at him while she had spoken but now she looked up at him. He looked amused and it greatly annoyed her, yet she kept that fact to herself.

"Really?"

"Well, duh. Why would I wanna make that up?"

"Maybe to get away from me!?" He suggested with a grin.

"Why? What are you gonna do? Hurt me? Yell at me? Laugh at me? Embarrass me? Try and make me do something I don't want to?" She forced a laugh. "Really. I don't think so. Now if I'm being very rude, excuse my behaviour, but I want to call a friend. I'll be back." With that she got up and hurried toward the payphone.

"No more then 5 minutes," he called softly after her. She ignored him. He couldn't understand her. He could've sworn he had seen anger, scorn, hatred, and hurt in her eyes when she had laughed at him. And that laugh, it had also been fake. He was sure of it. Well, he wasn't gonna sit here and wait for her, he was gonna be with her, just to try and find out what was up with her. He got up and followed her to the payphone.

She was just starting to dial the number when he got there. "What do you want here?" She asked, "I'm perfectly capable of making my own phone calls without a chaperone." She immediately regretted the retort. She was being harsh and without a reason. But still, she hated the fact that he had followed her. If she hadn't already put money in the machine, she wouldn't have called after all. But it was too late to back out now. She groaned and rolled her eyes as the phone started ringing.

"I know. And don't worry, I'll leave you alone." Steve grinned.

Just then Sandi picked up, "Hello."

"Hi, its me, Kate."

"Hey Kate, you back already? How'd your dinner go?"

"I'm using a payphone at a restaurant called Bridges, that's why you don't recognize the number. So what's up? You ok?" Sandi understood immediately that Kate wasn't alone and therefore had to be careful 'bout what she said.

"Yup, just I have a problem. You usually have good advice, so I thought I'd get your opinion." Sandi got straight to the point knowing her friend didn't have a lot of time to talk. Sandi explained that the guy she had been dating wasn't around much lately because of his job, and there was this other guy doing everything he could to separate the two of them because he wanted to go out with her. And then besides all that, there was another guy that she was really starting to like. What was she supposed to do? She still loved her boyfriend but she saw so little of him.

"Wow, you've certainly gotten yourself into a triangle of mess! That's not good! I don't know, girl. You're might have to talk it through with your boyfriend. He deserves to know how you feel. Sure, he might be angry and hurt at first, but if he truly loves you and you love him, he'll understand and forgive you. But I don't know, I'd have to think about it. Just don't do anything hasty." Kate shot Steve the evil eye as he stepped closer, so he quickly took a step back.

"Yeah, maybe. I'll think it over some more and we'll see. Just knowing you're standing behind me makes me feel better already. So how's school? Anyone find out bout your phone yet?" Sandi expertly changed the subject.

"Schools fine and no," Kate answered. She was very uncomfortable with Steve watching her every move, especially with the conversation turning towards their best kept secret yet, their cell phones. "Look, I really need to go, I'll call you again as soon as possible, k?"

Sandi wanted to argue with her. She hated it when Kate had to run off so soon, but she knew there was no use arguing. She sighed, "Alright, I'll be waiting. Bye!"

"Bye!"

Kate replaced the receiver back unto the hook, glared at Steve, shook her head and marched back to their table. Steve followed. "For a girl who never goes out, you sure give good advice." He remarked.

"Excuse me, but can't a girl have a little privacy anymore?" Kate demanded. Kate was already regretting being so mean to him. Even though she was tired, worried 'bout her friend, and had a splitting headache, she had no right to take it out on Steve.

"Why? Was that supposed to be a private phone call? Are you hiding something and you wanted to discuss it with your friend?" Steve was beginning to get angry.

"Look, I'm sorry, I have no right to be angry at you. It's just-, I just-, I'm just tired right now, and I have a headache. I'm sorry I took it out on you."

"What's wrong?" He looked genuinely concerned.

She didn't wanna tell him about her problems. They were none of his business. Yet—she found herself telling him all about Sandi's 3 guys problem, how her boyfriend worked so far away so he couldn't come home often and about this other guy that had come to mean so much to Sandi. "I don't know. What do you tell a friend when she needs help with something like that and you don't have a clue of what to do?"

"I don't know. I've never been in that kind of situation. But you should relax. She'll find her way through it all. You've got enough to worry about without worrying about your friends. Now what about you? Are you alright?"

Kate smiled, "Yeah, I'm fine."

'What a liar', he thought. Out loud he said, "Are you sure? You don't look too well."

"I said I'm fine." She said sharply.

"Ok, ok. I'm sorry."

Kate was too embarrassed to say anything. She couldn't believe she was acting like such a jerk to him.

Steve drove Cori, Miley and Kate home that night. It had actually been a fun evening for most of them. But that night her thoughts turned back to the problem of the disappearing trophies. Did Randi have anything to do with it? And if so, why? As soon as she had time, she would do a little investigating herself. She would try to find the trophy thief, and catch him or her too, and she would look into the handymen's background, if possible. She finally fell into a fitful sleep.

* * *

As time went on, Kate slowly let herself become friends (not close friends, but friends) with Steve, Cori, and Andrew. And because Steve, Andrew, and Cori all hung out with the cops, Annette, and Dwayne a lot, she became friends with them, too. They had fun together and the guys would often help them with their studies.

But there was one BIG problem, the trophies kept disappearing and reappearing in odd places. And one other thing had disappeared too, the key to Miss Rockheart's filing cabinet drawer where she kept the test answer keys. Only somebody who was writing the test would want those so they figured it had to be somebody attending the Boarding School. Right? Kate knew precisely who was behind it all, or at least she thought she knew, but it all didn't make any sense to her at all so she refrained from saying anything to anyone else. There were times when she felt like telling Steve but she wouldn't let herself. It was then that she would become distant from everyone, especially Steve. Those times would be hard on her friends.

Kate was always kinda wary of the cops and Cori, Andrew, and Steve, because she knew she was under suspicion of stealing the trophies. And lately she had come to suspect that maybe Steve, Cori, and Andrew weren't just handymen at the Boarding School. Maybe they were some kind of security guards. Or maybe even police men!? Could that be possible? Yes, she decided as she watched them with Dwayne and Annette, it could be possible and likely so. She didn't like it. And that feeling that told her the guys weren't really who they said they were also kept her from telling Miley of her decision to do a little investigating herself. And that was for two reasons: 1-she didn't want Miley to tell Cori and 2-she didn't wanna hurt Miley by telling her that her boyfriend was a fake, for Miley was finally sticking with him.

CHAPTER SIX

THE DECISION

It was in the beginning of December now and the Christmas Holidays were coming up fast. And so was the Christmas Party. Kate, Miley, Helen, and Annie had decided to sew their own dresses for the party during sewing class. They were coming along fine. The girls were also helping the others decorate the school. Halfway through December, the school was decorated from top to bottom. Even the guy's dorm had been decorated, with the girl's help, of course. The girls, all except Kate, were very excited about going home for the holidays. Kate was scared. Oh, sure, she was excited to see her family, but not excited to see some of her so-called 'friends' and her enemies.

But first before they could go home for the holidays, there was the Christmas party to go to. Steve had asked Kate to go with him but Kate hadn't given him a definite answer yet. Miley was going with Cori, of course. Helen had been asked by a guy named Mitch, and Annie was going with someone named Tony. Helen, Annie, and Miley were doing their best to get Kate to go with Steve, but so far Kate hadn't decided yet.

* * *

The alarm clock rang. Kate opened her eyes. 7:00 a.m. Her eyes traveled to the calendar. It was Friday, December 14th. There was only one more week until the party, which would be held on the 21st. This was also the day she had promised Steve a definite answer. She wanted to go with him, but could she? Did she dare? What if he was no better then the guys back home? Did she wanna go through that again? But then . . . would he do that to her to? He seemed like the kind of guy a girl could trust. But then so had the guys back home. And besides she didn't really know Steve, just the Steve he kept saying he was, the handyman. She couldn't risk that again. She would have to tell him no. Somehow, having decided against going with him didn't make her feel any better. She didn't want to go alone either . . .

She forced her thoughts to the back of her mind and got out of bed. Already she was in a bad mood. She glanced over at Miley, who was already getting dressed.

"Good morning," Miley greeted her with a smile.

Kate forced herself to smile back, "Morning."

"Today's the day, huh?"

Kate immediately regretted having told her friends what day she was going to give him a definite answer. "Don't remind me." She groaned. "I don't even wanna think about it."

"Have you decided?" Miley asked softly.

"I think so." Kate couldn't look at Miley. She knew she was going to disappoint her, "I don't think I'll go at all."

Just then there was a knock at the door. Kate slowly got up to open it. She was greeted by Annie and Helen. "Morning," They both greeted them with a smile. They, too, wanted to know what Kate had decided to do.

"Good morning," Kate and Miley answered in unison. "Come in."

Annie and Helen studied the other two, "By the looks of you two, I'm guessing you were talking about the party." Annie guessed.

Miley nodded, but Kate kept right on combing her hair.

"Oh no, you don't," Helen exclaimed. "Sit down, Kate. We're gonna have a little heart to heart here. Come on." Leading Kate to her still un-made bed, the three friends sat down together to try to persuade Kate to change her mind. "Alright, explain. Why not?"

They waited, Kate stared at the floor. She didn't know how to explain how scared she was of being hurt again. Of having every friend she had ever loved turn away every time she came near, because they couldn't bear to look at her.

"Hey, come on. You know we'll always stand behind you, no matter what. Why don't you just go with him and just have fun. Its only for one night. It doesn't even have to be a date, just go with him as friends." Miley coaxed gently.

"Yeah! And that way you won't have to go alone. And remember, Mrs. Mueller is expecting us there so you really don't have a choice of whether you wanna go or not." Annie added.

"And another thing is, if you don't go and another trophy disappears, or something else, someone just might frame you again, knowing that you weren't at the party." Helen reasoned. Kate had already been framed for two of the trophies that had disappeared. The thief was getting better framing her, too. The second one had been done so well, had it not been for Mr. Kennedy, the science teacher, who had seen Kate walk toward the big tree in the middle of the backyard and sit down under it to study just some minutes before it was discovered missing, she'd have gone down.

"Is everybody still expecting something to go missing that night?" Kate shivered.

"Yeah, but we're supposed to keep it quiet, remember? We don't want the thief knowing we're expecting him. Or her." Annie said, "And don't worry, nobody believes for even one minute that you're the one stealing them." But they knew that wasn't true. A lot of the students and some teachers always looked at her with that wary look in their eyes. It hurt her something awful. That was one of the reasons she couldn't sleep at night.

"And if you go with Steve, then he can help you prove that your innocent, because he'll be with you the whole time. Or, well, not 100% of the time, but at least he'll know where you are." Miley pleaded. Miley, Helen, and Annie were scared that the next time Kate would be framed, she wouldn't have a way to prove her innocence. And then she really would be in trouble and they had a feeling Kate wouldn't be able to go on anymore if that happened. She was hardly eating or sleeping as it was. If she looked like this when she went home for Christmas, her parents probably wouldn't let her come back.

"Alright, alright." Kate muttered, "I think I just made a major mistake though."

"Does that mean you agree to go?" Miley asked, barely holding back her excitement.

Kate took a deep breath, "Yeah, I'll go." The girls cheered and laughed. Kate held up her hand, "But only as friends and only on one condition." The girls immediately sobered.

"Anything," they breathed in unison. "Just so long as you'll go with Steve."

"Promise never to bug me 'bout him again." Kate ordered.

"We promise."

"Now help me get our room cleaned up and grab something to eat and get to class before we're late," They all laughed and hugged each other, thanking Kate again and again. Together they cleaned up the room again and got their stuff ready (as well as themselves) and hurried downstairs to eat breakfast.

Helen, Miley, Annie, and Kate were to meet Steve, Andrew, Cori, Mitch, and Tony for lunch that day. Kate was scared and nervous beyond words and try as she might, she couldn't concentrate on her work. She burned the sauce she was making in cooking class, spilled her science experiment, and not a single word her English teacher said registered. Nor could she remember a single word she had read. All three teachers asked if she was sick and if she wanted to go to the nurses office. Kate always declined, saying she was fine, just a little distracted. Each teacher would narrow his or her eyes and study her, and say, 'you don't look well at all, are you sure?' And when Kate would nod, they'd shake their head, sigh and say, "Then please try to pay more attention to what you're doing."

Miley, Annie, and Helen were all smiles, all morning long. For them the morning couldn't go by fast enough. But for Kate it was the other way 'round, the morning was flying by way too fast and before she knew it, that dreaded hour was here. RRIINNNGGGGG!!!! Kate jumped about a foot into the air as the bell rang. She knew it was lunchtime but she hadn't even been able to swallow any breakfast, and she certainly wasn't hungry now. She even considered pretending to be sick, when Annie grabbed her arm and, barely letting her snatch up her books, dragged her to her locker to get rid of her books and hurried toward the cafeteria. Kate almost had to run to keep up with her.

"Come on, Annie. Slow down. It's not like they're gonna run away or something." But she knew Annie wouldn't slow done till they had picked up their food and were seated at their table. She wasn't surprised to see Miley and Helen already sitting at their table. She and Annie had just sat down when the guys joined them.

Steve too had been nervous all morning about this meeting. He wanted Kate to go with him so that he could prove her innocent somehow and because he wanted to try and figure her out. She seemed to panic and then looked ready to cry or fight every time he or any other guy touched her. It didn't make sense. She was 17. What was wrong with her? The only reasonable solution he could find was that somebody must of hurt her bad. Or she must have lived in complete solitude and therefore wasn't used to that sort of thing (which was very unlikely since she and the other Minnesota girls were all very good friends).

The police force had even gone so far as to ask some of those that knew her back home. But everybody had said the same thing, "Anything you wanna know 'bout her, ask her yourself. If she wants you to know, she'll tell you." Except one guy had called her a few names (which we will not mention) and had immediately been slapped by more then one girl, punched by Kate's brother and threatened by her cousins and a few others. The police had then asked her brother, "Why all the secrecy? Are you hiding something? Or is she? Or are you all?"

The brother had said they weren't hiding anything, but Kate wasn't the kind of person that liked her life made known to everybody and anybody who wanted to know would have to ask Kate herself. And he had also threatened that Kate had better not be the worse for the wear either when she came back. That remark hadn't been very encouraging. Especially since she looked like she hadn't eaten or slept properly for weeks now.

Now as he approached their table, he studied the girls. Miley, Helen, and Annie were all smiles, talking and laughing excitedly. The funny thing was they were all grinning at him. Then he studied Kate. She looked like she usually did nowadays, unhappy and listless. She was pushing her food around on her plate. She had her head bowed, so he couldn't see her eyes. Miley elbowed her as the guys drew nearer and she glanced up momentarily. She had dark circles around her eyes and she looked like a scared rabbit! What was going on? He had noticed ever since she had been framed for the second time she had smiled a lot less, but he had never before seen her look this bad. She was positively trembling!

As they sat down, she glanced at them only long enough to mumble a greeting, then kept her head bowed. The others laughed and talked noisily for a while, but then, slowly, they all settled down and everything became expectantly quiet. This time Annie and Miley both elbowed Kate again. Kate took a deep breath and looked up. This time she had her eyes masked so expertly he thought he must have imagined that frightened look earlier on. When Kate didn't speak, Annie elbowed her again.

Annoyed Kate asked, "Can you puh-leease stop it? Honestly, if you keep it up, you're going to break my ribs."

"Sorry, just . . ." Kate shot her a look that said, 'Don't you dare!' And Annie was quiet. They all started eating again and the conversation started up once more. Ten minutes earlier then they usually left, the guys, all except Steve, got up and left. The girls followed immediately behind them, though Miley paused to squeeze her shoulder and whisper, "Remember, you promised." Even after they all left, Kate couldn't bring herself to lift her head.

Steve reached out and cupped her chin with his palm and lifted her face so that she had to look at him. He studied her face. It was unreadable. "What is it? What's wrong?" He asked.

She pushed his hand away and shook her head, "Nothing."

She was such a liar. He knew there was something wrong, but he also knew by the way her chin was set in that determined way that he'd get nothing out of her. So he decided to change the subject. "Have you decided whether you'll go with me or not?" He asked softly.

She nodded, "I'll go." It was said barely above a whisper and she kept her eyes on her still full plate. She stood up. "I-I have to go."

"But you haven't even eating your lunch yet." He protested. She merely shrugged.

"It don't matter. I ain't hungry." Then she turned and hurried away. Steve watched her go, more puzzled then ever.

Even thought Kate had given her word, she was still tempted more then once to tell him that she had changed her mind, but she didn't dare let her friends down like that. They were so happy now that she had said yes. She didn't wanna see them look at her with that worried look on their faces again and tip-toe around her like they were scared she'd break suddenly.

CHAPTER SEVEN

THE CHRISTMAS PARTY

And so the day of the party arrived. The girls had gotten that day off work and classes were only until lunch. Though the party only started at seven, Miley, Annie, and Helen dragged Kate and their dresses and everything else they needed to get ready for the party down to Jerry's right after they had cleaned their rooms after lunch. Jerry's was an old fashioned little restaurant. The Police usually went there to eat their meals or whenever they needed a break from work. There, they were going to meet Annette and Dawn, who had agreed to help them get ready for the party. Jerry's was located 'bout 10 blocks from the Boarding School, so the girls took a taxi.

Upon reaching Jerry's, they were ushered into a room in the back. It looked something like a sitting room with a set of sofas set in a semi circle on the far side of the room. One coffee table stood in the middle of the semi circle and another one on either side of the room. There were plants strewn here and there and a chess stood at the other end of the room, as well as a few other odds and ends, but Kate was too preoccupied to notice much.

They each took turns changing in the restroom. Though they had started early, it was nearly five o'clock by the time they were all ready. Annette and Dawn, along with Kate, Annie, Helen, and Miley had all promised to help with the last minute preparations with the party, and so together they went back to the Boarding School to help out. At about six the gym was as ready as it could get for the party and so the girls headed back to their rooms to freshen up a bit and to try and relax their nerves a little. They had never before gone to a dance like this and so they were all pretty nervous, though none as nervous as Kate. She had started to really like Steve and that scared her. She didn't want to like another guy again. It was just too risky.

Her thoughts rambled on, 'Well, I promised to go to the party with him and I can't back out now. But it'll have to end there. After the party, we'll both go our separate ways and forget we ever knew each other.' She decided. However, she didn't feel better now that she had decided that. Oh, well, she'd get over it, she was sure of that.

"A million miles away, huh, Kate?" Miley teased.

"Huh? What? Was somebody talking to me?" Kate flustered.

"Yeah, we were just saying that the guys'll be here any minute now." Annie grinned. "So me and Helen have to scoot back to our room. See ya."

"See ya," Kate flashed them both a smile as they left. Then turned to look at the time and was surprised to see that it was already ten to seven, the appointed time that the guys would be picking them up at their rooms to escort them downstairs. Just then there was a knock at the door.

"You ready?" Miley asked, shot her a worried look.

Kate smiled for Miley's benefit, "Yeah, let's do this, shall we?" But she let Miley open the door.

Steve and Cori both took a deep breath. "You wanna knock?" Cori asked.

Steve shook his head. "Miley will most likely be the one to open up anyway." And so Cori knocked and Steve had been right, Miley opened the door.

"Hi," She smiled. Then she looked over her shoulder and opened the door all the way. "They're here, Kate." Then she looked at Cori and grinned, "You look mighty handsome in a tux, you know? Shall we?" And while Cori blushed furiously, Miley took hold of his arm and together they went downstairs.

Kate came to the door then, biting her bottom lip. As she walked, he studied her. She was prettier then he'd ever seen her before. She was wearing a pale green dress with a darker green sash around her waist. Her skirt had a slanted ruffle halfway down which was also the color of the sash. Her sleeves were short and puffed with a thin dark green sash along the bottom. Her hair was done up in a messy bun with a few loose curls in all the right places around her face. She was stunning. He was speechless. He could see she was nervous, but then so was he. He wanted this night to be perfect. Kate smiled and he returned her smile. "Hi."

He stared at her, shook his head and smiled again, "You're beautiful, did you know that?" She looked away. She was about to make some sharp retort when she remembered the promise she had made herself. Since this was to be their first and last date she was gonna make sure they both enjoyed it.

So she looked up at him again and smiled, "You don't look so bad yourself."

He looked surprised then quickly smiled to cover his amazement. It wasn't everyday this girl handed out a compliment to guys. In fact he had never heard her give any guy a compliment before. "Thank you. Now shall we?" He asked holding out his arm. She put her arm through his and smiled. Together they walked back downstairs.

At the party, they danced to almost every song. She had forgotten how good it felt to have a guys' arms around her. They both had a wonderful time. But every time Kate was really starting to enjoy herself, she remember the promise she had made herself, which saddened and frustrated her. At bout eleven, they went outside to watch the stars. They sat together on the bench she had so often sat on to study. He looked at her and smiled.

"Did you have fun?" He asked. She nodded, "It has been a—a-," she searched for the right word, "I guess I could say a wonderful evening. Thank you." She wasn't looking at him. She was staring at her fingers in her lap. He gently took hold of her hands in both of his. She looked up at him. He smiled. She wanted to ask him how his evening had been but she didn't dare. She had a feeling she had gotten in too deep already. He leaned closer. She let him kiss her and couldn't help but kiss him back.

"I-I should go. I have to get up early tomorrow."

"You're plane is leaving tomorrow already?" Steve asked.

"Yeah, we have to be at the airport by 8:00."

"Let me walk you to your room," He offered. Kate let him. They were just about to enter the lobby when a movement at the other end of the room caught her eye. She tightened her grip on his arm and stopped, signalling for him to do the same. As they watched, a figure moved silently and quickly away from the trophy case. The figure disappeared through the side entrance of the lobby. Kate and Steve ran through the lobby to the trophy case. There, they discovered another trophy had disappeared. They raced out the side door, but by the time they got there, whoever it was that had just left through that door was gone.

"You think that might have been the thief?" Kate asked.

"Could've been."

"Or do you still think I'm the thief?"

"If that was any proof, then no," He smiled.

But she wasn't happy. She had known she was still under suspicion but she had hoped that by now that Steve, at least, would believe her. She tried to hide the disappointment on her face, but it was to late, Steve had already noticed it.

He tried to cheer her up, "Come on, don't be so down. Everybody's innocent until proven guilty."

"Yeah, whatever, I don't care. Whoever that was is long gone. I'm going to bed," Kate said, and with that she turned on her heel and ran up the stairs.

"Kate! Come on. I didn't mean anything by that." But she wasn't going to turn around and come back now. She was gone.

That night she lay in bed and thought. She thought of the missing trophies. Of the figure they had been to late to catch. The person they hadn't been able to make out who it was. The latest trophy to have disappeared. And of Steve. Of how she hated herself for liking him. Of how disappointing it was that he still didn't really believe her. And so many other things. She was thankful that she was leaving the next day. At least then she wouldn't have to be around everyone at the boarding school for a while.

CHAPTER EIGHT

WELCOME BACK?

She was back. Kate had mixed feelings about that. In a way she was glad, but in some ways she wasn't looking forward to being back. The reason she wasn't looking forward to being back was 'cause of the missing trophies and Steve. The reason she was glad to be back was 'cause life back home wasn't any better than it was here, thanks to her ex-friends. Well she wasn't going to leave here again until the trophy thief was caught, that much was certain.

Jane and Rachael came running out the front door as Kate and her friends stepped out of the taxi. Everything looked the same as it had about 4 months ago, yet how different it was now. They were no longer strangers, they belonged here now.

"Welcome back!" Jane and Rachael both greeted them with hugs and laughter. "My, how we've missed you all." Jane exclaimed.

"Yeah, no kidding. This place was quiet as a mouse with you all gone." Rachael grinned. "Bad news though, too." she added

Kate put up her hand, "Let me guess. No trophies disappeared."

"Yeah." They both nodded.

"But how'd you guess? Didn't we tell you to forget it till you got back? Has one day gone by without you thinking 'bout it?" Rachael scolded.

"Nope. And nothing you guys are gonna say is gonna make me stop thinking. Now tell me that the handymen and the cops are not around. I really don't feel like running into them today." Kate added, "And don't ask why."

"Well, you're in luck. They aren't around right at this moment, but they probably will come around soon again. Steve's been asking 'bout you." Rachael said.

"Let him ask. Let's go," she flashed them all a grin and hurried inside. The girls exchanged glances and followed her. Rachael and Jane helped them all unpack and after they were all settled, the girls, all except Kate, decided to go find the guys. When asked what they were to tell the others if they asked about her, she told them to tell them she was tired and needed some rest. Though that wasn't really true, she didn't wanna talk to them now. Not just yet. But she couldn't relax either. She wouldn't be able to relax until the real thief was caught. On the plane ride back to Dallas, she had run one idea after another through her head until she had one that made sense. She had to go to the police office. She would go see Dawn.

* * *

She stood in front of the building. DALLAS POLICE was written on the front of the building in big, bold letters. Kate jumped behind some bushes just as the front doors opened and somebody exited the building. She peered through the branches as they came nearer, and watched. She recognized Cori, Steve, Andrew, Annette, and Dwayne. She wondered why the handymen were there if nothing had disappeared. There was one other man and another woman with them whom she did not know. She couldn't make out what they were saying, because they were too far away. As soon as they left, she hurried into the building. Once inside, she timidly walked up to the front desk and asked to speak to Dawn. As the receptionist gave her directions to Dawn's office, she thought of asking her not to tell anyone she'd been there, but decided against it.

She hurried up a flight of stairs and down the hall to Dawn's office door. She reached up and knocked. Dawn answered her knock with a "Come in." As she entered, she noticed with relief no one other than Dawn was present in the office. "Well hello, Kate. So your back now, huh? How were your holidays? You happy to be back?" Dawn got up and gave her a hug as she greeted her with a parade of questions.

"Whoa!" Kate laughed, "One at a time, please. Yes, we're back. My holidays were pretty good and in a way, yeah, I'm happy to be back and in a way no, I'm not. But its too hard to explain so don't ask why its like that." After a little while of talking everyday talk, Kate got down to business. "Look, I came here for a reason and I'd like to get it over with if you don't mind. But 1st you've got to promise not to mention that I was here today to anyone."

"But why?" Dawn was confused and concerned.

"Because this is personal and I don't want anyone knowing about it. Not my Minnesota friends, not my Texas friends and not the cops either. And that includes Steve, Cori, and Andrew." By now she had it firmly fixed in her mind that Steve, Cori, and Andrew were not handymen, but Dallas police. Why else would they have been here? She had also overheard a conversation between the guys before she had left Dallas that had her convinced that the guys were cops. And she figured now was as good a time as any to find out for sure. Before she left this office today, she was going to know, not just think, but know, that they were cops.

"Alright, I promise. Go ahead."

"Well, I was wondering, if a crime has been committed, are you always notified? Or do they just call other cops?"

"Well, it depends. Cops usually only deal with the crimes in their areas. But if there is some big crime being committed that is too big for them to handle, then yes, they often ask us for help. Like, say drug dealing operations and there is other operations, too. And well, those dangerous operations that usually have millions of dollars involved. Usually it's the money that makes it so dangerous. You know what I mean?" Dawn watched Kate carefully as she spoke.

Kate nodded. "Yeah. Could you get me a list of all the cases that your office has helped or was notified of in say, the last three or four months?"

Dawn stared at her, wide eyed, "Why?"

"Like I told you, this is personal. Now can you, or can you not?" Kate's patience was wearing thin.

"Well, I doubt it, but I could ask my boss, Mr. Hans Cooper." Though Dawn knew full well they didn't ever do that, she had a feeling there was more behind this than a personal matter. Did this have anything to do with the thefts taking place at the Boarding School? If it did, maybe they could make a deal with her.

Kate thought it over a minute. Was it worth bringing him in on it, too? That meant she couldn't keep it a secret. But if she couldn't get that information from here, where would she get it from? Finally she agreed, "Alright, as long as he doesn't tell anyone either."

"I'll ask him not to. I'll go get him. Be right back." Dawn gave her a reassuring smile. After about 10 minutes, Dawn came back with her boss. Kate stood as they entered.

"Kathlyn, this is my boss, Mr. Cooper. Mr. Cooper, this is Kathlyn Farrell." They exchanged a greeting and Kate was asked to take a seat once again. The others also took a seat.

"So, Dawn here tells me you want some information about robberies happening in the last couple of months." Kate nodded. Mr. Cooper continued, "May I ask what you want it for?"

"Its personal."

"You're going to have to do better than that."

Kate sighed, "Alright, but I don't want anyone else knowing about this, ok?" They nodded. "When I got back to school earlier today, I was told that nothing had disappeared at the Boarding School while I had been gone. I knew that gave the police force all the more reason to believe that I was actually behind it. I'm sick and tired of being blamed for something I didn't do. And so I figured if I wanted to have my name cleared of that suspicion, I'd have to clear it myself. Now can you give me the information I need?"

"No one's blaming you. You have been framed and now we just have to prove that it wasn't you. But of what use would that information be to you?"

"Well, I figured if I was going to get anywhere, I might as well start at the beginning and get to the very bottom of it all."

"You mean catch the bad guy?"

"Yeah."

"Don't you think that's a little dangerous for you? I mean these criminals are usually armed. And besides, how is that information going to help you?" Mr. Cooper was still doubtful.

Kate explained patiently, "I thought maybe I could get some kind of link between some other robberies. Unless you can explain to me what good a trophy is other than to look at and feel proud of?"

"Well, you could use it to make copies of and sell them. You could also melt them down, and I'm sure there's more ways to use trophies."

"Well, we know they didn't melt them. Have you checked to make sure the ones that were returned are the originals?" Kate asked curiously.

Mr. Cooper chuckled, "Yes, we have. What kind of robberies do you think might be connected to it?"

"I'm not sure. I was thinking maybe something big. With big money involved. And throwing everyone off by taking trophies. I could be wrong, but its worth a try."

Mr. Cooper looked thoughtful for a while. Finally he focused his attention on her again, "I'm sorry, but it is a rule here that no one that is not working on a case in any way, does not have access to that information."

Kate sighed, "I kinda figured you'd say that, but it was worth a try." Slowly she got up and started toward the door. Suddenly she stopped and turned around again. "Before I go, I have just one more question."

Mr. Cooper nodded, "Go ahead."

Kate hesitated. "Well, I've been wondering this for a while now and I finally convinced myself that its true. The Boarding School's handymen are really Dallas police, right?"

Both Mr. Cooper and Dawn were caught off guard, "Now who told you a thing like that?"

Kate pointed an index finger at her head and said, "My brain told me."

"And why would your brain tell you something like that?"

"Because its smart." Kate laughed, but she quickly sobered, "I see I'm right. And I was so hoping that those three were who they said they were. Especially Cori, for Miley's sake. I hate when a guy lies to my friend."

"Whoa! Now, just hold on a minute. We never said it was true." Mr. Cooper interrupted.

"And you also didn't say that it wasn't true. But that look on your faces gave you away." Kate smiled politely.

"What look?" Dawn asked curiously.

"That carefully guarded look on your face."

"Alright, alright. Who told you?" Mr. Cooper asked.

"Nobody. I just figured." Though that wasn't exactly true, she didn't want to tell him that she'd been spying on the handymen.

"Have you been spying on them?"

"Well, I have overheard a conversation or two between them, yes, but I can't exactly call that spying."

"Well, that figures. The way I see it, you have two choices. Either you're going to work with us or you're working against us. You know what I mean?" Mr. Cooper smiled.

"Yeah, you're pretty much saying either I help you catch this thief or I am this thief." Kate narrowed her eyes. She shook her head, muttering,

"People these days." She thought it over for a minute, "Alright, I'll work with you but only on one condition."

"What condition is that?" Mr. Cooper asked.

"Miley is in on it, too. What I mean is, I can tell Miley anything I want, when I want, about the whole thing. And she can help me if she wants to." Kate said firmly.

Mr. Cooper thought it over, "You wouldn't tell anyone else then that Steve, Andrew, and Cori are really cops?"

Kate smiled, "Nope. Not if I can tell Miley."

"Alright, you have a deal." Mr. Cooper held out his hand, and Kate shook it with a smile.

"Now I want you to wait here 'till our police friends get here." Mr. Cooper picked up the phone and started dialing as Kate took a seat once more.

* * *

While Kate had been getting herself a deal at the police office, Miley, Annie and Helen had been getting reacquainted with all their old friends at the Boarding School, including the handymen. Steve was just about to head inside to find Kate when his cell phone rang.

"Hello, Steve Parker speaking." Steve answered it.

"Parker, I need you and the rest of the gang to get back to the office immediately. And bring Miley Johnson with you." Mr. Cooper ordered.

"What? What's going on? And why Miley?"

"Never mind why or what. Just get over here. And don't forget to bring Miley."

"Yes sir. We'll be right there."

He put his phone back in his pocket and looked around for the others. "Hey guys, I need to talk to you for a minute." And so Cori, Andrew, Annette, and Dwayne walked a little ways away from the others and Steve told them what their boss, Hans Cooper, had told him.

"Sounds like trouble." Cori said thoughtfully.

"Well, let's go." Annette replied grimly. The others nodded in agreement and together they asked Miley to come with them to the police office. "Why?" She asked. They explained that Mr. Cooper, Annette's and Dwayne's boss, wanted to see her. With everybody wondering half a dozen questions, they hurried to the police office. Once there, they were surprised to see Kate seated in one of the chairs going over something on the computer with Mr.

Cooper and Dawn. When they entered, Mr. Cooper nodded at Kate. She returned his nod, and stood to her feet.

"Miley, can I talk to you in the hallway for a minute, please?" Kate smiled at her friend.

Miley noticed that though Kate was smiling, her eyes weren't happy. But then again she couldn't remember the last time that Kate had actually looked completely happy. It seemed something was bothering her. Even when they had been back in Minnesota something had been on her mind. Whenever she asked Kate about it, Kate always said it was nothing. She silently follow Kate into the hallway. "What is it?"

So Kate explained why she had come there in the first place.

"I came here because I knew they could tell me a few things that would help me find the real thief. But you see they didn't want to give me that information. I guess they still doubted me too much. And so I was about to leave when I remembered this certain suspicion about our Boarding School's handymen I had had for a while and so I asked Mr. Cooper 'bout it today and found out I was right. Do you want me to tell you about it or would you rather hear it from Cori?"

Miley was confused and worried, "You tell me."

"We better sit down first." Kate glanced up and down the hallway and saw what looked like a sitting area not far away. Thankfully, it was empty. She led Miley to a seat and sat down beside her.

"You see, for a while now, I've been wondering if Steve, Cori, and Andrew really are the Boarding School's handymen." Kate searched for a way to soften the blow.

"Of course they are!" Miley interrupted.

"Just listen, ok? In a way they are. They fix things at school every now and then. But, in truth, they are police men." Kate waited to let the news sink in. Miley looked away and jus sat there for a long time.

Miley turned to face Kate again, "Really? Honestly?" Kate nodded. "So Cori lied to me?"

"Only because I had to." Neither girl had heard Cori walk up behind them. "I'm sorry, Miley. Really, I am." Kate immediately understood the look Cori sent her way and she slowly got up.

Cori caught her arm as she passed him, "Steve wants to talk to you. I think he was a bit upset that he didn't get to welcome you back and that you didn't talk to him 'bout this 1st."

Kate forced a smile, "Ok, thanks." And with that she hurried down the hall.

CHAPTER NINE

GETTING STARTED

Kate entered Dawn's office without knocking.

Mr. Cooper smiled at her, "Is she ok?"

"Give her time and she'll be fine." Kate answered.

Steve scowled, "Was it honestly necessary to bring her in on it, too?"

Kate's eyes hardened, "Yes, it was."

"Why couldn't you have just kept her out of it instead of giving her such a hard time. And what's this going to do to her relationship with Cori? They were happy together." Steve was angry. "And why couldn't *you* stay out of it?" He knew he shouldn't be yelling at her like this. If the whole thing was the other way around, he would've told his best friend, too.

"Calm down, Steve. You know as well as I do that there's nothing wrong with telling Miley as long as she tells no one else. And you also know that's not why you're angry." Andrew scolded.

Steve shot him a dark look, but he kept quiet. Kate glared at Steve and then turned her back on him. And so, in angry silence, they waited for Cori and Miley to return. Thankfully, they didn't have to wait long. Cori and Miley returned with their arms around each other. Miley gave Kate a reassuring look as she sat down.

"Alright, I don't have all day so lets get started. Miley, do you promise not to tell anybody who Steve, Cori, and Andrew really are? As well as any information about these crimes?"

"Yes, sir." Miley nodded.

"Alright, first I want you both to tell us everything you know about these robberies."

"Miley doesn't know anything. I didn't tell her anything." Kate said quickly.

"Is that true, Miley?" Mr. Cooper wanted to be perfectly sure there was nothing crooked about these girls. He didn't quite trust them yet.

"Yeah. Its true." Miley said quietly.

"Ok then, guys, Kathlyn here thinks that whoever this thief is might be throwing us off the real catch by stealing trophies at the Boarding School. She figures this thief has some real big thing going on and he, or she, knows that the cops will be busy trying to track down the trophy thief and therefore have a better chance of getting away with the big catch. Kate, did you find anything in the computer?"

"Well, not exactly. You can do background checks on people, too, right?"

"Yes, but what are you getting at?"

"Well, do you know a Millard Miller?" Kate ignored the question and asked one of her own.

"Never heard of him. Why?" Mr. Cooper asked.

"Look him up. I overheard Randi, Mel, and Lori talking about doing something for a Millard Miller. Whatever they were doing didn't sound good. They didn't sound like they enjoyed doing it but they couldn't stop now because Millard would turn them over to the authorities and they were getting paid good money for it, too, by the sounds of it."

"How long have you known this?" Mr. Cooper asked.

"Since before the night that Andrew, Cori, and Steve took us to dinner. Andrew asked us then if we knew anything. Well I did, but I didn't want to tell anyone until I was sure of what was going on. And besides, I didn't trust any of you guys. I didn't want anyone else to be suspected of theft when they had nothing to do with it. But I think they kinda suspected that I had overheard some things they had said and they made sure not to speak of things like that outside of their room or at least not anywhere near me anymore. And so I didn't learn anything else, but I had a name. And that's why I came here today."

"Alright, you guys know what to do. Get everything you can about this guy. And check out Randi's, Lori's, and Mel's backgrounds as well. Cori, take these girls back to the Boarding School and then you get back here and help out." Mr. Cooper ordered. "I have to go now. I have some work to do myself."

"Wait a second. I kept my end of the deal. You can't just send us out now that you have everything you need!" Kate protested.

"Sorry, girls, but this kind of work is too dangerous for you. Just keep the information coming." Mr. Cooper smiled apologetically. And with that, he left the room.

"Sorry, Kate, but I have to listen to my boss. Lets go." Cori said gently.

"If that boss of yours thinks I'm actually gonna let him do that and still help him out, he's got another thought coming." Kate declared, eyes blazing. And she marched angrily from the room.

Later on that evening, she lay on the couch in the library wondering what she should do. Cori had assured them that they would be kept up to date. But the only way they were allowed to help was if they overheard something, they were supposed to tell the police immediately. 'Well, not gonna happen. They don't keep their end of the deal, I don't keep my end. But I can't really do anything without knowing how to defend myself. Hmmm . . . . lets see. Maybe I could ask one of the cops to teach me. But which one? Well, I'm definitely not asking Cori, and I don't really want a guy teaching me, so I'll ask Annette. If she won't then I'll ask Steve. But I'll have to let him cool off first. And I won't take no for an answer.' With that in mind, she sat up to study her History.

"I thought I might find you in here." Kate hadn't heard Mrs. Wilder come into the room and she jumped when Mrs. Wilder began to speak. "I'm sorry. I didn't mean to scare you." Mrs. Wilder smiled and sat down beside Kate.

"That's ok." Kate returned the smile. She and Mrs. Wilder were good friends and Mrs. Wilder usually let her get away with more than any of the other teachers, though she could be very strict too. Mrs. Wilder also seemed to understand her better then anyone else.

"Something bothering you?"

"You always see right through me, don't you?" Kate smiled ruefully.

"Your eyes don't lie." Mrs. Wilder smiled.

"Well, I just got a little upset 'bout something and now I'm trying to figure it out." Before long Kate found herself telling her friend and teacher all 'bout her problem.

"Well, I understand why you so badly want this person caught, but it wouldn't look good for the police force if they let you help with the investigation and you got hurt. You have to understand that they're just doing it for your own good and for the good of their reputation."

"Yeah, I guess so."

"Remember, they don't want you hurt. They want what's best for you, and you ought to want what's best for yourself, too."

"Yes, ma'am."

"Now, I think its time for bed for both of us. I know I'm tired and you look drained. What do you say?"

"Alright, and thanks for listening, I appreciate it." Kate smiled.

"No problem. I'm always here for you. Now, good night." Mrs. Wilder grinned, her eyes sparkling.

"Good night, Mrs. Wilder."

* * *

Two days later, she found herself in the workout room of the Police building with Steve. Annette hadn't had time to teach Kate and so she had begged Steve to teach her. It had taken quite some coaxing but finally he had agreed. An so day after day, he taught her. Many arguments came with those lessons. He would beg her to stay out of it and she would shut her mouth tight and not speak to him at all. He got very frustrated with her and often threatened to quit teaching her. But she had made it clear that whether or not she could defend herself, she was going to catch this thief, and so it was better if she could defend herself. He was amazed that her grades didn't suffer more then they did and he always wondered when she found the time to study. And so one day, when she asked him to teach her an extra hour, he decided to ask her.

"But Kate, when do you find time to study?"

"In the evenings and mornings."

"How early do you get up then? And how late do you stay awake?"

"Do you ever run out of questions?" Kate asked, exasperated.

"No, I guess I don't."

"Well, lets start working on it again. Oh, and by the way, you haven't told anyone 'bout this, have you?"

"No, stupidly, I haven't told anyone."

"Good, just keep it to yourself. Or you know what'll happen."

"Yeah, yeah." He muttered, glaring at her.

She gave him a sweet smile and started practicing again. He had to admit she was getting pretty good at it. But he didn't like what she wanted to do and he wished he could stop her somehow. He would just have to come up with a plan.

Miley couldn't believe Kate was actually serious about this. She wished Kate would just leave it to the police force. It was too dangerous for her. But Kate was determined and nothing was going to change her mind. It was Saturday night and Kate was in the gym 'keeping in shape' while Miley was in their room getting ready for a party. Miley was going to go with Cori. Though Steve had asked her to go with him, Kate had politely refused, saying she needed to study for an upcoming exam.

Miley looked at herself in the mirror. She sighed, not because of the image staring back at her, but because Kate wasn't coming with her. She wished everything would go back to the way they had been in the beginning of the year. At least then Kate had had time for her friends. Now she was too busy for anything except her schoolwork and keeping in shape. And she was barely getting her schoolwork done either. She hardly ever laughed much anymore and her smile had long since lost its beautiful sparkle. She always had that subdued look on her face like she was deep in thought.

Miley picked up her purse and hurried out of the room and down the stairs to the gym. She stood just inside the door watching Kate for a while before Kate noticed her.

Kate's thought ran through her head faster than she was running. If they weren't so mixed up, maybe she could concentrate on catching the thief. Why did thoughts of Steve, Cori and Miley and all the fun they used to have run through her head again and again? She couldn't think about that right now. She had to concentrate on coming up with a plan to get the thief cornered. Suddenly she saw movement in the corner of her eye and stopped running. Thankfully, it was only Miley.

"Is this what your gonna do all night?" Miley asked.

"No, I could never run that long," Kate smiled.

"Then what are you gonna do all night?"

"I plan on getting a little information. But please don't tell Steve or Cori. You know how they are."

"No, I don't know how they are." Miley replied coolly.

Kate looked at her in surprise, "What's wrong? Why upset?"

"Look, I'm sorry. Its just that you used to have time for your friends. Now you're never around anymore. I wanted to go to this party with you and Steve and Cori. Why won't you go? It won't be any fun without you. Kate, please come!" Miley pleaded.

"I'm sorry. I can't!"

"Why can't you?"

"Well 1st, I already told Steve I wasn't going and 2nd, there's something going on tonight that'll give me more information and tonight is probably the only night I'll get that information."

"Why do you need this information? Why can't you just leave it to the police? I can't believe this case is more important to you than your own friends!" Miley cried.

"Hey, come on, it's not more important than my friends. Its . . . its just . . ." Kate didn't know how to explain without letting information slip that she didn't want to tell anyone.

"Its what? Its just so important that you can't wait one more day to get the information that you supposedly need?"

"If I could, I would wait one more day and then I would go with you. But Randi's having her party today, too." She immediately regretted telling Miley that.

"Oh, so you're going to Randi's party instead of your friends' party? You know what? That's just great. Do what you want. But do be sure to let us know once friends mean something to you again." And with that, Miley turned and ran from the room.

Kate called to her, but Miley kept running. Kate didn't run after her. She stood where she was, wondering if maybe she had gone too far. Had she taken this whole thing too far? When she thought it over, she couldn't remember the last time she had gone out with her friends just to have fun. Unless school or the mystery of the disappearing things had been involved, Kate had lately turned down every plea to hang out and have fun. She had only been on one outing since Christmas. Though her friends had often begged her to join them when they went out, she had always declined.

Well, maybe she could stop in at the party on her way back from Randi's house. Kate had overheard Randi, Lori, and Melissa talking about the party that Randi was going to have at her house tonight. Kate had not been invited and nor had many other students from the Boarding School. In fact, Kate didn't know of anyone that had been invited and that made her suspicious. She wanted to find out who was invited and why nobody that she knew of from the Boarding School was. She was determined to get to the bottom of this. She was a little frightened to go on her own but since no one was supporting her in any way, she had decided not to tell anyone what she knew. She knew it could get dangerous, especially if this party was of the people responsible for the robberies, but she didn't care. With that in mind, she headed up to her room to get ready.

Kate was wearing black jeans and a brown shirt with a black leather jacket over it. She had pulled her hair into a ponytail and was heading down the stairs when she almost ran into Steve.

"Whoa, Kate! Slow down. Where are you off to in such a hurry?" Steve asked.

Kate smiled, "You know me, I'm always in a hurry."

"But your not always dressed like that when your hurrying off someplace. By the way, you look great." He smiled, almost sadly.

Kate blushed, "Thanks. But, no, I'm not going anywhere special. Just going for a walk."

"I don't think it's a good idea going for a walk dressed in black at this time of night."

"Don't worry 'bout me. I can take care of myself."

"Are you sure some guy isn't gonna be taking care of you?"

Kate stared at him wide eyed, "Steve! Honestly. Are you out of your mind? Of course not. Nobody takes care of me. I'm taking care of myself. And I aint going on a date either."

"What's so all-fired important that you can't go to the party with me?" Steve asked.

"Not you, too." Kate groaned, "It just that I'm really not in the mood to go to a party right now, ok? Nothing personal."

"No, that's not it. You are so not a good liar, you know?"

Kate sighed, "So I've been told. But I seriously don't feel like going to a party tonight." She wished he would just go away so that she could go, but he was blocking her way down the stairs.

"Come on, it would be fun. We don't have to make it a date, we can just go as friends."

"Its not that. I just don't wanna go at all. I'm sorry." Kate whispered.

Steve sighed, "Did you know you are the most stubborn person I have ever met?"

"You've told me that a time or two before. Now, please, can you let me through?"

He stepped aside but caught her arm as she stepped past him, "Are you sure you're just going for a walk?"

"Look, Steve, I said I was going for a walk and I am going for a walk, ok?"

Steve grinned, "Ok, I get it. Would you mind some company? I have a few more minutes before its time to go to the party."

"I wouldn't mind, but its kinda a soulful walk. I hope you don't mind."

Steve nodded, but the smile had left his face, "I understand." Kate nodded slightly and hurried down the stairs and out the door.

CHAPTER TEN

BUSTED?

As soon as she was out of sight of the Boarding School, she fished Randi's address out of her pocket. It hadn't been too difficult getting the address. She had asked Mrs. Mueller at the office. Though convincing her that she was studying for the upcoming exam with Randi in the evening had been a little tough. She explained that she had misplaced the address Randi had given her and Randi had already left so she hadn't known where else to get it from.

But Mrs. Mueller knew that the two girls did not get along at all, so she didn't believe her. That is, until Kate explained that she and Randi were trying to get over their differences, and they had decided that studying for the upcoming exam together would be a great way to start. So finally Mrs. Mueller had believed her and given her the address. Randi lived bout 15 blocks northeast of the Boarding School so Kate had decided to walk halfway around the block and go with a Taxi from there. And that is just what she did. But she told the Taxi driver to let her off two block prier to reaching her destination.

As she got out of the Taxi, she began to doubt the wisdom of going alone and she wished Steve were with her. It was already beginning to get dark and she was acutely aware of it. She was so nervous, that she didn't even notice how cold it was. But she shoved all thoughts from her mind and hurried down the street. She hadn't come this far for nothing. There was a park across from Randi's house and she planned on hiding out there until the party got into full swing. And so she made herself comfortable on a bench in the middle of the park where she still had full view of Randi's place. For a long time she watched as vehicles full of people arrived in droves. She wished it weren't so dark out so that she could try and recognize somebody. But it was no use. Oh well, she'd find out soon enough. When people would stop arriving, she'd go check it out.

* * *

Quietly, she got up off the bench and headed round the block. She intended to make it look like she was just going for a walk and then head down the alley behind the house and find out what was going on. But as she got nearer, she saw she had a problem. There was a tall solid wood fence 'bout a foot higher than her head surrounding the property in the back of the house.

Great! Now, what would she do? Just as she was about to give up and go back to school, she noticed a piece of wood on one of the boards had been broken off near the ground. It was perfect! She could spy through that hole without being noticed by anyone that happened to pass by.

An elegant yard filled with people met her curious gaze. Some were playing a croquet game, others were watching. There was a refreshment stand at one end of the yard and she could see some people had a whiskey drink in their hand. She noticed the back doors of the house were opened and guest were entering and exiting all the time. That meant the party was not just an outdoor party but also an indoor one. She thought this would make it harder to find Randi and her friends, but as she watched, Randi, Mel, Lori, and some guy came 'round the corner of the house and headed inside.

Her legs were getting tired so she changed to a sitting position. Suddenly she heard a rough male voice behind her, "Gettin' kinda comfortable there, ain't ye?" She froze. Her blood ran cold. Her hands felt clammy and she had goose bumps on her arms and neck. Suddenly she felt very vulnerable in the dark alley. She tried to push the feeling aside but it insisted on staying, crowding her mind with many horrifying imaginations. She suddenly realized just how stupid she had been to come here alone. She wished Steve were with her. Or she should've just forgotten the whole thing and gone to that party with her friends. She could be having loads of fun with her friends at that very moment and here she was in a dark dangerous alley in the middle of Texas with an unwelcome stranger behind her. She pinched herself, hoping to wake up and find it all just a horrible nightmare but she knew even before he spoke again that it was for real. When he spoke again, he was closer, "Are ye deaf?"

Slowly, ever so slowly, she turned around. With her sitting on the ground, he looked huge. And scary. Thankfully, the light was behind her, so he couldn't see her face. But that, too, in a way, added to her disadvantage for that meant she could see his face clearly and it wasn't a pretty sight. "Who are ye?" He asked. "And what're ye doin' here?"

Slowly she stood to her feet. Even when she stood, he towered above her. He was a big man with even bigger muscles and she knew this was not the kind of guy to mess with. He had a long scar down one side of his face. Without the scar he wouldn't have been half-bad looking, but the scar gave him that tough, scary look. She took a deep breath. "No, its not exactly comfortable, the ground's kinda cold. And no, I aint deaf, neither." She paused. She had to do some fast thinking, something at which she was usually not very good at.

He grinned, "An' my other two quest'ens?" He asked between puffs of his cigar.

"Well, umm, you see, I'm uh, part of this band and we were supposed to play for somebody at one of these houses along this street tonight and I was supposed to meet my band there, but I forgot exactly which house it was." She took a deep breath. "So I was gonna see if the rest of my band was here. And if they were, I'd go join them."

He snorted, "So that's why ye're sitting here, spyin' on us? Do ye 'xpect me to buy that?"

She shot him an exaggerated look, "And why not?"

"If ye really are a part of a band and ye were s'pose to play somewhere, ye'd just call them and find out where they are."

"What would I call them with? I ain't got a cell phone."

"Ha! That's even funnier. Everybody owns a cell phone."

"Well, this girl doesn't."

"Why don't ye tell me who exactly 'tis girl' is? And why she don't jest go to the door to find out if her band is playing here?"

"Because if it wasn't at this place, then I'd have to leave right away and that would be rude."

"An' spyin' on us ain't rude?"

Kate's eyes grew wide with pretend astonishment, "Oh, my! Of course its rude. I'm sorry, sir. I hadn't even thought of that before. I'm not so bright sometimes. If you'll excuse me, I'll try to find another way to find my band."

"Oh no. Ye ain't goin' nowhere. Ye are gonna come wit' me and we are gonna go see if your band is inside. If it ain't, ye are gonna get more than ye bargained fer. And ye ain't leavin' 'til ye tell me who ye are and why ye 're really here." With that he grabbed her by the arm and marched her toward the gate.

Suddenly, someone jumped out from seemingly nowhere and hit the stranger with his feet.

"Get out of here."

Though it was too dark to recognize the newcomer, Kate immediately recognized his voice. It was Steve!

She hurried out of the way, but refused to leave without Steve. Steve and the other guy fought for a while and Steve knocked him out just as a few guys entered the alley from the party. Steve and Kate both raced from the alley. One of the newcomers stayed with his friend but the others chased them. Steve had parked his car just outside the alley and so they quickly hopped in and took off just in time. Thankfully the chasers didn't follow them further.

When they were well out of the neighbourhood, she spoke, "Boy, am I ever glad you showed up when you did. But how did you know where I was?"

For a while, Steve said nothing. But finally he answered her question, "I didn't."

"Oh." Kate was surprised, but said nothing further. They drove in silence until they got to the Boarding School. Even after Steve had parked the car and they were heading inside, he still wouldn't say anything. He marched her up the stairs to her room.

"Unlock it." Steve ordered grimly.

Kate did as she was told and together they went inside. Once inside, Steve closed and locked the door. It was then that he started talking. Angrily.

"What in the world were you thinking?"

"Calm down, ok? I was thinking I wanted information."

"Have you no sense at all? What has gotten into you?"

"Yes, I still have some sense. What has gotten into me?! You know full well what has gotten into me." Kate was starting to get really annoyed with him.

"No. I don't know what has gotten into you. You really went too far this time. From now on I don't want to see you anywhere off the school's premises. Is that understood?" Having said that he turned on his heel and left the room angrily. As he left, Kate heard him muttering, "Part of a band?! Is she crazy?"

Kate didn't learn until later on in the following week that she had just blown a major investigation planned by the police. The following week also turned out to be very eventful, and not very pleasant.

On Monday, she failed her science test. On Wednesday, she couldn't find her favourite running shoes for gym class and barely passed her math test. But Thursday was the worst. 1st she overslept, making her late for class, and it seemed nothing was making any sense at all in her schoolwork. She was usually a pretty bright student and caught unto things quickly, but Thursday it was just about impossible to figure anything out.

She groaned in frustration and rested her head in her hands.

"Kate, is there something wrong?" Miss Rockheart asked during History class. Miss Rockheart had never liked Kate much. Kate did not have a good memory and so she wasn't the greatest student in her class. Miss Rockheart didn't exactly care about Kate's health and the only reason she asked was because she knew Kate would say she was alright. At least that's what Kate thought.

Kate looked up, "Umm, no. I'm alright." Under her breath she muttered, "I think."

"Well, if you're alright then get your work done. We haven't got all day. Or do you think you have special privileges?"

Kate just glared at her teacher. Kate knew how Miss Rockheart felt about her and therefore cared little about her either.

As if the day hadn't already been bad enough, she got called into the principal's office after class. When she knocked on Mrs. Mueller's office door, the door was opened by Mrs. Mueller.

"Kathlyn, come on in." As she entered, she noticed Steve and Cori were also in the room. "Take a seat." Mrs. Mueller invited her to sit down in the sitting area with the guys and herself. She immediately noticed they were all facing the television set. She was really beginning to wonder what was going on. None of the others looked at all happy and she had a feeling it wasn't going to be good.

"We want to show you something." Cori said, turning on the TV. They all watched in silence. It didn't take Kate long to realize they had videotaped her room.

She gasped, "You guys videotaped my room? That's how you show this trust you supposedly have in me?"

"Kate, if you were obeying the rules and keeping yourself clean and out of trouble, you wouldn't have to worry 'bout us having videotaped your room. Now would you?" Steve remarked sarcastically.

Kate groaned, but said nothing. She watched herself enter the room and lock the door. She sat down on the bed and even on TV you could see she had been crying. Kate barely dared to breath, for she knew what was coming. She watched herself reach inside her demin jacket and bring out her cell phone. Her cell phone and those of her friends were the best kept secret in the Boarding School. She couldn't believe they had done this to her. She watched angrily as she dialled Sandi Reiley's number in her phone. Kate remembered that Sandi hadn't picked up that day. She had made the phone call on Tuesday. It had been Tuesday that she had learned from Miley 'bout the investigation that never happened because she had been there and Steve had had to help her out. Now she was glad Sandi hadn't picked up. But she hated herself for using her cell phone at all. She should've known they'd tape her room sooner or later.

From the tape, the cops and Mrs. Mueller learned how little she slept, how she paced the room at night, how she worked on her schoolwork when thinking was making her ready to scream with frustration whether it be day or night, how she would often sit miserably on her bed and do nothing at all for long periods of time, and most importantly, they learned about her cell phone. By the time they stopped the video, she was resting her head in her hands in defeat.

"So young lady, would you like to explain all this?" Mrs. Mueller asked sternly.

Kate shook her head.

"Then we have a few questions for you." Mrs. Mueller said.

Cori started with the question she most dreaded, "Who's cell phone is that?"

Kate sighed. She wished she could lie about it, but she knew there was no use. They would find out sooner or later. "It's mine."

"How long have you had it?" Cori asked.

"Umm, for about a year now, I think."

"How long have you had it here at school?"

"For as long as I've been here." Kate knew there was no use lying.

"So you had it here even before Christmas?" This question came from Steve.

"Yeah, I did." Kate answered quietly.

"What do you use it for?" Steve asked.

"To chat with my friends and family back home."

"Who were you trying to call Tuesday?" Cori asked.

"Sandi Reiley."

"And who is she?"

"She's the girl I told you 'bout before Christmas on that business date thing." Kate directed her answer to Steve.

Cori looked at Steve, "Do you remember her?"

"You mean the girl you called that night?" Steve asked Kate.

"Yeah, her." Kate was surprised Steve remembered. She hadn't expected him to.

"I see. Where's your phone now?"

Kate hesitated, taking a deep breath. Slowly letting it out, she finally answered quietly, "In my pocket."

Steve held out his hand. Standing up slowly, she slid the phone out of her pocket. She weighed it in her hand. Stepping toward Steve, she handed it to him.

"We're gonna have to go through this." Cori told her.

"Be my guest."

"Well now, lets see. If you told us everything that's in it, maybe we won't have to search it?" Steve said it more like a question than a comment.

Kate laughed at him sarcastically. "You expect me to believe that?" Do you really think that I still don't know that you guys don't exactly trust me. Even if I told you exactly what's in my phone, you would still search it 'cuz you wouldn't believe me."

"No, we wouldn't. Then we would hand the phone over to Mrs. Mueller here, and she could do with it whatever she thought was best." Cori argued.

"No thanks. Look for yourself."

Steve shrugged, "Ok. We'll be handing it in to Mrs. Mueller once we're done with it.

Kate was being stubborn again and Steve hated it. Why couldn't she just cooperate for once. Why did she always have to have things her way? Did she really realize in just how much trouble she'd be in if something incriminating was found in her phone? Why didn't she trust him? After all, he had helped her secretly when he would've gotten into big trouble if his boss had known. And she had blown that investigation they had been counting on.

Mrs. Mueller spoke up, "And another thing, Kathlyn, your grades have been falling quite fast. And far, too. There is one thing you must remember, your parents are paying good money for you to go to school here, whether you like it here or not. You don't want to let them down by failing, or worse, getting expelled, do you? They are counting on you to make them proud. Think about it."

Kate sighed, "I know, I know." She leaned back and closed her eyes.

"If you know that then I suggest you go back to doing your schoolwork the way you did before Christmas. Leave this case to the police. Its their job. Your job is to make the people that care about you, and that you care about, proud."

She knew they were right. She knew she should do as they told her, but she hated giving in to others. But she had no choice. She had to give in. "Ok, ok. I promise to stay away from the case and work harder on my grades if you promise that I'll be the first to know, outside of the police force and Mrs. Mueller, when you find the thief. And you'll let me have a little privacy when I need it."

"Consider it done." Cori smiled.

"It better be." Kate grimaced, shaking her head. "Now can I go? I haven't exactly had an excellent day and I'm exhausted."

"So I've heard. Yes, you may go." Mrs. Mueller remarked.

Kate nodded her thanks, and headed for her room. As the door closed behind her, Cori whistled softly, "What a girl."

CHAPTER ELEVEN

INNOCENT

Over the next few weeks, with Miley's help, Kate got her old job back as a waitress at Arby's. She also brought her grades back up to her former high scores. She went with her friends wherever they asked her to, and within a few days Helen and Annie were once again talking to her as well. They no longer acted as if she were some stranger they didn't know.

"You know, Kate, its good to have you back." Miley smiled. It was Saturday. The girls had been shopping all morning and had decided to eat at Arby's for lunch altogether before they had to go back to work. They were sitting in a booth close to the entrance of the restaurant.

Kate laughed, "I've been here all along."

"True, but for a while there, some weird stranger kidnapped you or something, and took your place. I'm glad that stranger finally decided to go away and leave us with our awesome friend, Kate Farrell, once more." Annie grinned

"Cheers." Miley was happier than anyone else that the old Kate was back once more. She had missed her a lot. And why wouldn't she? They had been best friends since fifth grade.

Kate looked at Miley, then glanced at the other two girls. She smiled, "Well, its good to be back. I can't believe I missed out on all this for one dumb case."

Though Kate called it a 'dumb case', Miley knew how badly Kate wanted these guys caught so that she could be herself again without having to worry. Miley, too, hoped it wouldn't take the police long to find them now.

Just as they were finishing lunch, Steve and Cori entered the restaurant. Without waiting to be seated, they headed right towards the girls.

"Hello there, girls."

"Hi," the girls chorused.

Steve and Cori quickly got chairs from a nearby table and sat down at the end of the booth.

"Oh my, Helen. Look at the time. If we don't run, we'll be late for work!" Annie suddenly exclaimed.

"Uh oh, we'd love to stay and chat, but we gotta go. Thanks for an awesome morning, you two." Helen added.

"Good bye, have fun." Miley and Kate waved as they hurried off to work.

Steve grinned, "I hope you two aren't gonna rush off on us yet, too!"

Miley laughed, "Nope, at least not yet. We still have some time."

There was a short pause in the conversation and the girls noticed the guys kept grinning at each other.

"What makes you two so happy?" Kate asked curiously.

Steve looked at Cori and Cori looked at Steve, "You tell 'em." Cori said with a smile.

"Well, we've got some good news." Steve smiled.

"And then some bad news." Cori frowned.

"Are you ever gonna tell us or are you gonna keep us guessing?" Miley teased. Kate waited quietly and somewhat warily. She usually didn't like any kind of news and didn't know whether to be scared or excited.

"If you keep quiet long enough, we'll tell you," Steve laughed. "We caught the thief."

Kate gasped, "Honestly?" Then she narrowed her eyes, "You're not just fooling with me, are you?"

"Honestly, Kate. I'm not fooling. You're off the hook for good. Innocent!"

"Oh, Kate, that's so wonderful. I'm so happy for you." Miley laughed in excitement. Congratulations made their way around the table.

"Since when?" Miley grinned.

"Since yesterday." Cori smiled.

"Thank you, guys. I appreciate it." Kate smiled. "Tell us about it."

"Well, you remember Millard Miller?"

The girls nodded.

"He was behind it alright, but you were barking up the wrong tree trying to find the middle man." Steve told Kate.

"What do ya mean?"

"You know how you were sure that Randi and her friends were the ones doing the job for him?"

"Uhhuh." Kate nodded.

"Well, they worked for him, alright. But not that. They didn't have a clue what was going on. Their job was to show up at each and every one of his many parties and keep the guys entertained."

"Wow, what a job! How did they entertain them?" Miley asked.

"Singing, dancing, things like that." Cori explained.

"So if it wasn't them, then who was it?" Kate asked.

"That's part of the bad news." Cori said. "Are you ready to hear it?"

"How come I get the feeling I ain't gonna like this at all?" Kate groaned. Then she added, "Yeah, I'm as ready as I'll ever be."

"Ok," Steve took a deep breath and watching Kate's face closely, said, "Jannette Armstrong."

Kate turned pale, her eyes grew wide for a second, and then she closed her eyes, leaned back against the back of the seat and groaned, "Not her."

Miley gasped, "You mean our Jane? The hair stylist?"

"I'm afraid so." Steve said quietly. "I'm sorry, I wish it could've been different."

"Yeah, me too." Cori added.

After a short silence, Kate asked, "What's gonna happen to her?"

"Well, we're not sure yet. She won't be going to the Boarding School anymore, that's for sure." Steve said.

"I see."

"The other part of the bad news is, we haven't found Millard yet." Soon after that the girls had to get back to work. They both received a hug from each of the guys. The guys, being very sympathetic, offered to stay with them the rest of the day, but the girls kindly refused.

Paying attention to their job was hard for both of them, but Steve and Cori had told Rhonda what they had just told the girls and so Rhonda took it easy on them. She even asked if they would like the day off, but the girls had declined.

After work, they had to explain their long faces to Annie and Helen. And once again, first came the congratulations, and then came the disappointment when discovering they had been betrayed by a good friend.

The next day, Steve found Kate in the library, just staring at the floor. Steve cleared his throat, for he didn't want to scare her. She jumped anyway.

"I'm sorry. I didn't mean to scare you." Steve said.

"No, its ok. Don't worry 'bout it."

"Mind if I sit down?"

"No, I don't mind. Go ahead."

Steve sat down a few inches away from her on the couch. "How are you feeling?" He asked softly.

"I guess as good as can be expected for someone who lately learned that the person she thought was a good friend whom she could trust just happened to be the complete opposite."

Steve took her hand and squeezed it, but said nothing.

"Steve?"

"Yeah?"

"I'd like to talk to her. Could I?" Kate asked hesitantly.

"Are you sure?" Steve asked softly.

Kate swallowed hard, then nodded, "Yeah, I'm sure."

"Ok, sure. As a matter of fact, she's been asking to talk to you. I just wasn't sure I should bring it up."

"Ok, so when?"

"Whenever you're ready."

Kate smiled slightly, "Right now?" she asked.

"Alright, lets go." He put his arm around her shoulders and together they left for the courthouse.

"Nervous?" Steve asked. They had reached the courthouse and were headed toward the cell Jane was being kept in until the trial.

Kate grimaced, "Yeah."

Jane was sitting on her cot and staring at the floor when they got there. For a moment, she didn't notice them. But when she looked up and saw her visitor, a saddened, embarrassed look fell over her face.

Kate reached for the door and looked at Steve. She didn't have to speak, for Steve knew what she meant. He unlocked the door and followed Kate into the cell. For a while Kate just stood there gazing at Jane. Jane couldn't gaze back into her eyes; she looked away.

"Why, Jane?" Kate whispered.

Jane glanced back at her, then started pacing. "I don't know. I—I just—I'm sorry."

"I thought we were friends. I liked you. I—I trusted you!" Kate exclaimed.

Jane hung her head. She knew Kate's trust had to be earned. Kate didn't just trust anyone. She had often wished that Kate didn't really trust her, for she knew she would one day be found out and Kate would know she had betrayed her.

Kate asked Steve for some alone time with Jane, assuring him she would be fine. He promised to be just outside the door if she needed him.

"Jane, please tell me about it." Kate pleaded.

"I can't. You'll tell Steve and he can't know."

"You haven't told the cops anything yet?" Kate was surprised.

"No, and I don't plan to either." Jane replied sharply.

"Ok, look, I promise not to tell them. So, please tell me?"

"How will I know you will keep your promise?"

"Jane, I trusted you. Now I'm asking you to trust me. I swear it'll be off the record."

"Ok, ok. It all started when I met this guy Millard at a nightclub a month or so before school started. We started dating. At 1st it was great, but when he wanted me to spend more time with him than I really had time for, and at all hours of the day or night, I didn't want to do it. I told him I couldn't spend all my time with him; that I needed to get my schoolwork done yet, too. So, he told me if I wanted to be his girlfriend, I'd have to do as he said. And after an argument like that he would always be so sweet, kind, and considerate, and that would make me feel guilty for upsetting him. But after a little while, it'd be the same again. He'd control my life and order me around until I'd get really upset again. And so on." Jane sighed.

"It seems when I told him I needed time to get my schoolwork done, and what school I was attending, he got an idea. As it turned out, he had once gone to the Boarding School here and had been expelled by Mrs. Mueller." Jane explained.

"For doing what?"

"Doing whatever he wanted, when he wanted, breaking every rule in the book, bullying and failing in all subjects, and so on."

"Wow!" Kate said wide-eyed.

"Yeah. Anyway, he still had this huge grudge against Mrs. Mueller, and wanted to pay her back. So I let him talk me into doing all his dirty work for him, like stealing and framing you."

Kate groaned, "Oh no."

"I'm sorry. I never meant to hurt you like this. Its just that in the beginning, when this all started, I didn't know you and well, it was Millard's idea to frame the new girls. He thought it would be a nice practical joke on Mrs. Mueller for accepting students from so far away. And since I didn't know you, I didn't mind. It seemed to make him happy and proud of me and l wanted him to be happy. I also wanted him to be proud of me. It was also Millard who got the idea to get to know you so you'd let me into your turf so it'd be easier to plant the stolen items." Jane sighed.

"At first I loved it. He was happy, and that made me happy. But you made getting to know you tough and in a way, that was even better, because since you were so distant people would easily believe you were the thief, and that's why I mostly framed you." She continued, "But in a way, it was awful, 'cause the harder you made it, the more I liked you. And then as I got to know you and your friends, I started to like all of you. Being with you girls was so much fun. So I told Millard I didn't want to frame you anymore, and on occasions I didn't, but Millard threatened to turn me over to the authorities if I didn't."

"But if he was in on it, then wouldn't he have gotten in trouble, too?" Kate asked.

"No, he would've denied it and made sure he had a sure way to keep his name clear." Jane sighed.

"You have to tell the cops. You need to turn over this Millard guy. Then they can help you get a deal with the D.A. Do you know where he might be?" Kate coaxed.

"Remember, you promised not to say anything." Jane warned.

"Yes, I promised, and I'll keep that promise. But I still think you should tell the cops. I mean, you know this guy. You could help them find him. And, Jane, think 'bout it, if you don't help them and they don't find him, you'll still go to prison, but he'll go unpunished. And you won't ever be able to finish school, either." Jane just stared at the floor miserably.

"They have enough evidence to put you away for a long time, but if you can give them Millard, and tell them what you told me, I'm sure they'll cut you a deal." Kate kept trying to convince Jane.

Just then Steve knocked on the door and stuck his head inside, "Hey, umm, Kate, we're gonna have to head back soon."

"Just give me a minute, ok?" Kate barely glanced at him.

Steve shrugged, "Alright." And closed the door again.

Neither girl said anything for a little while. Finally Jane spoke, "Why do you want me to do this anyway? You should be glad to see me go."

"Jane, I know you. You're my friend, remember? You're the girl that was so excited to graduate. And you only have a few weeks left 'til graduation. You're the girl that wanted nothing but a little fun. You're still young. And besides, you were put up to it." Then she sighed, "Yes, it'll take me a while to understand; to forget and forgive, but that doesn't mean I want you to throw your future away. You still have your whole life in front of you. So think about it, ok?"

Kate got up from where she was sitting on the bed beside Jane, "Well, I have to go now, so good luck."

"Thanks. And thanks for stopping by." Jane didn't dare look at her. It was as if the girls had forgotten that one had framed the other while speaking, but now as they parted, they seemed to remember, and therefore were both distant.

Kate was quiet as she and Steve left the courthouse. She had so much to think about and everything was so jumbled and confusing, she was getting a terrible headache.

"So how'd it go?" Steve asked. He had been waiting for Kate to talk about it voluntarily, but when she didn't, he couldn't help but ask. He was curious. He hoped Jane would've told her something of Millard's whereabouts, or something else that might help them. He didn't doubt for a moment that Kate would tell him all 'bout it. He had watched them from outside the cell for a while and had noticed both girls talked quite a bit. So they must have been telling each other something.

Kate took a deep breath and slowly let it out. "It went fine." She felt a sudden strong urge to cry. She struggled to keep her emotions under control.

After a moment of awkward silence, he asked, "What were you two talking about?"

Kate gave him a wry smile, "It's confidential."

"What do you mean confidential? She told you 'bout Millard, didn't she?"

"Yes, she did, and that's why it's confidential." Kate answered.

"Come on, Kate. You can help us nail him." Steve petitioned.

"You don't need my help. Jane will help you." Kate argued.

"You know as well as I do that she ain't talking to us, so how can she help us?" Steve argued.

"Go see Jane tomorrow, or maybe the day after, and I'm sure she'll be willing to talk." Kate replied calmly. "Now, can we please drop this conversation? I have a headache." She leaned her head back and closed her eyes.

"Alright, alright. I rest my case." Steve grumble. Kate smiled. Steve hated it when he had to give in to Kate, especially when it was about the case.

CHAPTER TWELVE

THE CASE IS CLOSED

Later on, at the dinner table, the four girls all sat at their usual table together. Though all of them had been thinking about Jane all day—worrying about her, questioning her actions, resenting her, and feeling sorry for her—they tried to talk about other things for Kate's sake. But Kate couldn't pay attention to their chatter, her mind kept going back to the conversation with Jane earlier on. During a lull in the conversation, she blurted, "I talked to Jane today."

"Really?"

Kate nodded.

"Where?"

"At the courthouse." Kate answered.

"What'd she say? Or what did you guys talk about?"

"Well," Kate thought for a moment. She hardly knew what she could tell the girls and what she couldn't. But since she had brought it up, she had to tell them something. "We talked about the case, I guess you could say." Kate put up her hand just as the girls were about to ask more questions. "Don't ask me about it 'cause I promised her not to tell anyone. But she did say to tell you how sorry she is for doing what she did."

"If she's so sorry, why'd she do it?" Miley grumbled. "You know, if she hadn't done it, she wouldn't have to be sorry, and she wouldn't be sitting in the courthouse right now."

"And we wouldn't be sitting here discussing this right 'bout now either." Helen added.

"Yeah." Annie agreed.

Kate explained, "Girls, I know right now you don't understand. I didn't either, not until I talked to her. Now I know her side of the story as well as our side, so I understand why she did what she did. And you will, too, soon. I hope it works out for her. Anyway, I have to go. It was nice having lunch with you."

The girls nodded, staring at her in disbelief. They couldn't believe their ears. Was Kate seriously going to forgive Jane this quickly? Had she really become that easily trusting, gullible person once more like she used to be? Or was something wrong?

They were still sitting in dismayed silence when Steve and Cori walked up, "Hey, girls, something wrong?"

The girls blinked, shaking their head to clear it.

"I—I don't know. I hope not." Miley stammered.

"What do you mean 'you don't know'? And where's Kate?" Steve demanded.

"She just left." Annie replied.

"You see, she just told us she had talked to Jane today, and she was all understanding and wishing her well. It ain't like Kate to be so understanding and forgiving so quickly. At least not the Kate she's been for the past year or so, anyway." Miley explained.

"Yeah, so we were just a little worried about her." Helen added.

"Kate talked to Jane?" Cori asked, surprised.

"Yes, she asked me to take her to Jane earlier today, so I took her down to the courthouse." Steve informed him. "From what Kate told me, I know Jane told her everything about the case, including things we want to know, but she said she couldn't tell me. Did Kate mention anything to you that might help us?"

Miley sighed, "No, she said she had promised Jane not to tell anyone."

"Ok. And when you said 'at least not the Kate she's been for the past year' what did you mean with that?" Steve asked, curious.

"Well, Kate used to be really carefree, and well, you'd never see her without a smile on her face. That was until some jerks took advantage of her carefree teasing, laughing ways and got her in deep trouble." Helen blurted.

"Helen! Kate will never forgive you if she found out you just told them that." Annie said wide-eyed.

"She's quite right, Helen." No one had heard Kate walk up behind them.

"Look, I'm sorry, Kate. I—It's just that I didn't think you would mind, now that your proven innocent and all." Helen stammered.

"Really? And what does my being proved innocent have anything to do with my personal life or my past?" Kate demanded.

Helen hung her head, "Nothing."

"Look, I know you mean well, but when it comes to my private life and my past, please let me be the one to tell others about it. And let me decide who needs to know 'bout it as well."

"Yes, Kate. I'll remember that." Helen said quietly. For a while no one spoke.

Finally, Steve asked, "Kate, don't you think we would be able to understand you better if you told us?"

"Are you sure you're worried 'bout understanding me, or arresting me?" Kate asked, an angry glint in her eye. Suddenly, not being able to stay serious, she burst out laughing and gently pushed him. He was so surprised, he didn't know what to say.

"Look, Helen, I'm sorry. I didn't mean to be so hard on you. You forgive me and I'll forgive you, deal?" Kate asked with a soft smile tugging at her lips.

Helen grinned, "Deal!" They gave each other a great big hug.

"Alright, lets go sit down in the library, I'll tell you about it." Kate informed them.

So once everyone was in the library, she started her story, "I was 15 and loving life. I could make everyone laugh at a dumb joke pretty much anywhere, anytime. No matter where I went, I was usually the life of the place, laughing and talking. I could be real mean, but just as easily, extremely nice.

"Since I was old enough to start thinking about dating guys, they have been asking me out all the time. I was used to that kind of thing. What I wasn't used to was being stalked. That happened when I was 15. There were these two guys, they both wanted to go out with me, and, well they were disgusting and perverted, so I turned them down. But they didn't wanna take no as an answer, so at first they stalked me, following me everywhere. When that didn't work, they threatened me. They said that if I wouldn't go out with them, they would hurt me bad. But they never said what they were going to do to me. Turns out it wouldn't have changed anything even if I had gone out with them."

"When I still wouldn't go out with them even after they threatened me, they suddenly stopped following me and I didn't see them for about two weeks, so I thought I was rid of them. But then one day, they robbed a bank, the same bank I have an account at. It was an inside job, so it was easy for them to make it look like me and a few friends had done the robbing. So I was put in prison for a month or so, until the guys made a mistake and some cops caught them and proved me innocent."

"The thing that hurt the most was that all my friends, except for these three, actually believed that I was the thief, and no matter what the cops said now, I was an ex-convict and nothing was going to change that. So they all, especially the guys, ridiculed me and made fun of me whenever they got the chance. So my whole life seemed to flow down the drains from then on."

"Wow, that must have been tough." Steve said sympathetically. Both Steve and Cori understood Kate a lot more now.

"Kate, tell them what mistake the guys made." Helen coaxed gently.

"Ok." Kate swallowed. "Before I was out of prison, the same two guys came to visit me. They were laughing and asked if I wanted to go out with them yet, seeing as to how they would probably be the only guys I'd ever be able to kiss after this. So I asked them if they had been the ones that set me up, but they denied it, laughing.

But in prison, I hadn't totally lost my sparkle yet, so I had tons of friends, and one of the other inmates heard them laughing at me and quickly got rid of them." Kate said with a grin. "After that visit, I started thinking. I strongly believed the guys were the thieves. So I asked for a meeting with my arresting officer and told him about the visit, as well as how they had stalked and threatened me before it all happened. So he promised me he'd look into it and to this day, those guys are sitting in my former cell, with tons of enemies on both sides.

"Actually, I asked the other inmates to be nice to them, that they had already been punished, so I'm guessing by now they have a few friends." Kate laughed.

"Wow, I guess I can see why you dislike guys so much." Steve said wryly.

* * *

That night, as Kate lay in bed, she hoped and prayed with all her heart that Jane would talk to the cops, and tell them what they needed to know.

She was glad she had gone to talk to her. Though it had been somewhat difficult, it had paid off. She now not only understood Jane's situation, she had also forgiven her. Though it would still be hard to forget it for a while yet, she knew it was going to be ok. She felt as if a heavy burden had been lifted from her heart and as if she were living on air, light as a feather. Needless to say, she hadn't felt this wonderful in months.

For the first time in months, she slept like a baby. When she woke up the next morning, she felt refreshed and ready to go. Somehow, she knew everything would be alright.

All day, she paid close attention to her classes, trying to catch up on all the information she had lost lately. She passed the surprise test in mathematics with flying colors. The brownies she made in cooking class were so good, all the students and teachers wanted a piece. But because she wasn't good at remembering things, she had a tougher time in history class. But Kate was determined not to fail History, or any subject for that matter, and therefore worked hard all day to get caught up. And she was determined to work hard to rest of the year as well, to ensure that she'd get a passing grade.

Miley, Annie, and Helen also helped her out wherever they could. The week continued smoothly for the girls. Mrs. Mueller was spending extra time with Kate, helping her with those subjects she was behind in.

All week, the girls heard nothing from the boys. They didn't call, nor did they stop by. Kate was starting to get worried so she finally asked Mrs. Mueller if she had heard from them, but she hadn't, either. So there was nothing they could do except wait, hope, and pray.

Kate sighed. It was Friday night, and she and the girls were all spread out in the library. The others were reading, but Kate was studying. Miley heard her sigh and asked if she was getting tired of studying. Annie and Helen looked up as Miley spoke, and listened.

"It's not that. I mean, I wouldn't be getting tired of studying if I could actually pay attention. But I can't pay attention." Kate frowned.

"Well, what's bothering you?" Though Miley knew what was bothering Kate, she asked anyway.

"You know what's bothering me," Kate muttered.

"It's the boy's, isn't it?" Miley asked softly.

"And Jane?" Annie added.

"Yeah, why haven't they said anything yet? Where are they? What are they doing? Has Jane told them yet? I'm worried, really worried." Kate said.

"I don't know. We all are." Helen replied.

"Yeah. But it'll be alright. We just got'ta think positive." Miley tried to comfort not only Kate, but also herself. She, too, was worried about her friends.

"Yeah, Miley's right. And besides, those boys know what they're doing, and they can take care of themselves, so don't worry." Annie agreed.

"Its getting late, we should all go get some sleep. Kate, you've had enough studying for one day, you need some rest, too." Miley smiled. "And who knows, maybe we'll hear from the boys tomorrow."

"That's true. Lets go." Kate smiled gratefully at her friends, and together they headed for their rooms.

* * *

It was already 8:30 a.m. on Saturday morning. Miley smiled contentedly as she glanced toward Kate's bed in the mirror. Though it was somewhat past their usual wake up time, Kate was still asleep, and Miley didn't plan on waking her up anytime soon, either. She herself had only woken up a few minutes ago. Still in her pyjamas, Miley was brushing her hair slowly, thoughtfully. It was nice to see Kate sleep so peacefully again. For a while there, it had seemed as if Kate had always been working, or busy doing something else, even when she was sleeping. Now a smile danced across her lips from time to time. Miley was lost in her thoughts when she heard a light knock on the door.

Brush in hand, she walked lightly to the door and opened it. She stared wide eyed, dropping her brush on the floor. She stooped down to pick it up.

"Cori, you're back!" She remembered just in time to be quiet so as not to arouse Kate. Cori greeted her with a hug and a kiss.

"Yeah, we're back." Cori grinned. "Did we wake you?"

Miley laughed, "No, I've been awake for a little while now. Just haven't gotten dressed yet. I guess I didn't expect any visitors this morning."

"Ok good, Steve's with me, too. Can we come in?" Cori asked.

"Morning, Steve." Miley smiled at him. "Yeah, you can come in just so long as you promise not to wake up Kate."

"Don't promise her anything, guys. Its too late, I'm already awake." Kate interrupted with a grin. The boys entered the room.

"Good morning, Kate. Sorry we woke you." Miley apologized.

"Morning. Are you kidding? It's a good thing you woke me." Kate smiled. "Morning, guys."

"Good morning, sleepyhead." Steve teased.

"Good morning." Cori greeted her.

"What brings you here this morning?" Kate yawned.

"Well, you know, maybe we should just come back later, once you're fully awake." Steve loved to tease Kate, especially when he was in a good mood.

"Don't you dare go anywhere till you tell us all about it." Kate threatened, but she was smiling.

Steve and Cori looked at each other. "Where do we begin?"

"Well, you could start by taking a seat. And then you could continue by starting at the very beginning of the week, namely Monday." Kate grinned.

"Well, alright. Since you insist." The guys sat down beside Miley and Kate on their beds. Then they brought the girls up-to-date on the happenings of the past week. They told them all about how Jane had told them everything she knew about Millard. And with that information, they had had more than enough evidence to put him in prison for a very long time. So the cops had arrested him, as well as his accomplices, all during the week. Since Jane had helped them catch the shark, she was off the hook and free to do as she liked. Well, not entirely as she liked, she was on probation.

"So the case is closed, huh?" Kate murmured.

"Not quite. But it will be as soon as he's been to court, which ain't too far away." Cori smiled.

"What is Jane gonna do now?" Kate asked.

"She didn't know yet." Steve answered softly.

"If she's clear, than why doesn't she come back to school?" Kate asked curiously.

"I don't know. I'm not sure Mrs. Mueller would let her come back even if she wanted to." Steve informed her.

"Why not? I mean, sure, she stole some things, but that wasn't really her fault, and besides, she said she hadn't wanted to do it. Millard made her." Kate said. "And quit staring at me like that."

Steve, Cori, and Miley were all staring at her wide-eyed. They sure hadn't expected that from her. They quickly turned their attention elsewhere when she told them to stop staring. They all shrugged, not knowing what to say.

"Will you guys come with me to talk to Mrs. Mueller? Maybe we can change her mind." Kate asked.

They glanced at each other and shrugged. Cori answered, "I guess it couldn't hurt."

"But don't you think you two should get dressed first? It might help if you're not wearing pjs when we try and persuade Mrs. Mueller." Steve teased again. They all laughed.

"Yeah, yeah." Kate grinned.

"Then why don't you two get on out of here so we can change?" Miley said, still smiling. The boys left the room laughing. The girls quickly changed, washed up, brushed their teeth, and combed their hair. In less than ten minutes, they joined the boys in the hallway, who pretended to be extremely shocked that the girls were ready so soon.

"Don't you girls want breakfast first?" The boys asked, as the girls headed for Mrs. Mueller's office.

The girls grinned, "Nope, not till after."

The guys shrugged, "Whatever."

Kate knocked on Mrs. Mueller's office door.

Mrs. Mueller invited them in. She was busy doing some paperwork at her desk when they entered.

CHAPTER THIRTEEN

JANE RETURNS

"Good morning, Mrs. Mueller." They all greeted her with a smile.

"Why, good morning. What can I do for you today?"

Since it had been Kate's idea, she started, "It's about Jane."

"What about Jane?"

Kate explained, "Well, I was wondering if she would be coming to school here again?"

"Oh, I see. Well, you don't have anything to worry about. She won't be coming back." Mrs. Mueller smiled kindly at her.

"Actually, I was kind of hoping she would be coming back." Kate explained patiently.

Mrs. Mueller was puzzled, "Now why would you want her around when she has caused so much trouble for you already?"

Kate swallowed, "I don't know. I guess it's 'cause she was a good friend. And, well, I feel sorry for her. She was really looking forward to graduating, and it just doesn't seem fair that she can't just because she let some guy influence her." After a few more minutes of reasoning back and forth, Mrs. Mueller agreed to let Jane come back to school. Kate forgot all about eating breakfast as she and Steve got to be the ones to tell Jane.

Jane was shy at first and didn't seem to be interested in coming back to school, but Kate coaxed her to, telling her that she wanted her to come back.

"Even if you want me to, everyone else will hate and despise me, not that I blame them." Jane moaned.

"No, Jane, listen. Now everyone knows how you've been framing me and putting me in trouble all the time, right?" Kate asked.

Jane sighed, "Yeah."

"Ok. So, when they see me hang out with you and we both forget the whole thing and act like nothing ever happened, they'll forgive you, too."

"I don't know, Kate. I mean, I'll never forget what I did to you. Its just so awful." Jane was beating herself up inside, and Kate hated it.

"Jane, stop it!" Kate exclaimed. "Forget it, ok? What's done is done. You can't change what happened. You can't go back from here. What you can do is, either you stand still, beating yourself up, or forget and forgive yourself, and move on. So what's it gonna be? Now I have a plan that'll help you if you want to come back to school, and trust me, it'll work."

Jane thought for a long time. Finally, she agreed to come back to school so she could graduate. So Kate filled her and Steve in on the plan. They both loved it and agreed to it immediately.

Her plan was that Jane would not come back to school until the Easter dance, which was to be held at the end of next week. Until then, Kate would bring her all her homework and help her catch up. That, of course, would have to be done during the hour and a half between school and her job that Kate usually spent doing her own homework.

Then, at the dance, Kate, and maybe her friends, including their dates, and Jane, would wait until the dance was in full swing, then, altogether, they would join the dance so that everyone would see Jane was amongst them as a friend. Meanwhile, until the party, they would spread the fact that Jane was planning on coming back to school, just to warn the students. They would also make sure the students knew that Kate was ok with the fact that Jane was coming back.

So once Kate and Steve got back to the Boarding School, they filled Mrs. Mueller in on the plan, too. At first, Mrs. Mueller was very shocked that Kate would want to help Jane like that, but when Kate assured her that she seriously meant it, she was quite pleased with the plan and extremely proud of Kate. And so therefore, agreed to it whole-heartedly. She told Kate, "I am so proud of you for doing this. It really is very kind of you. I'm sure Jane truly appreciates this."

The rumour that Jane was coming back to the Boarding School spread like wildfire, and by the middle of the week, everyone knew about it. They also knew that Kate didn't mind that Jane was coming back. Many of the students told her how crazy she was to have forgiven Jane like that. They always asked her why, but for a while, not wanting to talk about it, Kate denied them an explanation. But eventually, she became tired of ignoring them. So she told them a bit of Jane's situation, and how, having everyone around you give you that strange look and give you the cold shoulder had made her feel. She explained that she never wanted anyone else to have to feel that way, and so that was why she had forgiven Jane.

All week, Kate brought Jane her homework assignments, and helped her do them. Kate did everything she could to make sure Jane got caught up in her work. But since Kate spent so much time helping Jane with her work after school, that meant she had to do her homework at night. So every night, after coming back to the school from the restaurant, tired from a long day, she would do her homework. Thankfully, she did some of her homework during lunch and during any other chance she got, which helped a lot. And she and Jane did a lot of their homework together, so she usually didn't have to stay up any later than 11 p.m.

* * *

Steve entered the library during lunch hour on Friday. It was empty except for a few students here and there. He couldn't see Kate anywhere so he asked Mrs. Wilder if she had come in. Nodding, Mrs. Wilder showed him where Kate was, working on some of her homework, in the very back corner of the library.

Steve greeted her pleasantly as he approached her, "Hey, Kate. How are you?"

Kate looked up, smiling when she saw him, "Hi. I'm doing fine. How 'bout you?"

"I'm fine. Are you sure you haven't bitten off more than you can chew again?" Steve asked. "Your friends are starting to get worried about you."

"What do you mean? I'm taking good care of myself. I have a good job with a healthy environment, do all my schoolwork, help out Jane, and sleep. No, I haven't bitten off more than I can chew. The only thing I don't have time for this week is going shopping, or whatever else, with my friends. And, that is going to change after this week." Kate said confidently.

"Ok, ok. I get it. Just make sure you take it easy every once in a while." Steve smiled wryly.

Kate smiled. "I promise to try not to forget." She said, laughing. "Now, if you don't mind, I need to get back to my homework." Then she turned her attention back to her books.

"Here, let me help you with that."

Kate smiled gratefully at him.

* * *

Kate yawned. She glanced at herself in the mirror one more time. Her peach-coloured, knee-length dress made her skin look a few shades darker than it really was. She was a little tired, but she was sure she's be able to stay awake until after the party. Right now, she had to hurry down to the library. They had all agreed to meet there.

Miley, Cori, Steve, and Jane were already there when she entered the library. After greeting each of them, Kate took a seat on the empty chair beside the love seat, which was where Steve was sitting.

Jane suddenly blurted, "You know, I'm gonna feel really weird, being the only one without a date, and going to a dance with four other couples."

"Whoa!" Kate exclaimed defensively, "In case you haven't noticed, Steve and I are NOT a couple, and we aren't exactly going together as a-well-as a date." Kate blushed furiously. She was just about to continue, when she was saved by the arrival of the rest of the gang.

"Who says you don't have a date? We asked you to dress nice for a reason, you know?" Annie laughed. At that moment, Ryan Bartley stepped out from behind the others. Ryan had had a crush on Jane practically since the day he met her.

Ryan got down on his knee in front of Jane, "Could I have the pleasure of escorting you to the dance?"

"Why, absolutely." Jane was extremely happy. Her life was starting to look and feel normal again.

And so, as it turned out, Steve and Kate were the only ones not going as a couple. After a few minutes of chatting, they all headed for the ballroom. The other students weren't entirely surprised that Jane came with Kate and her friends. At least not all of them. Most of them accepted the fact that Jane was back and even welcomed her.

Kate loved to dance and sing, and she did so for a while, but after about an hour of singing and dancing to every song played, she was beginning to get really tired, so she stayed on the sidelines and chatted with the others. Except, she did dance with Steve to a slow song.

"So we didn't come as a couple today, did we?" Steve teased.

Kate immediately blushed, "Just forget it, ok?"

"Why? Don't you wanna talk about it?" Steve was loving it.

Kate narrowed her eyes at him, and shook her head, "No, sir, I don't."

Steve chuckled. He held her close, whispering into her hair, "You know, if I had believed for one minute that you'd come as my date, I'd have asked you."

For a moment, she let herself relax in his arms, but she couldn't resist arguing, "No, you wouldn't have."

"Now, how do you know that?" Steve asked.

"Because you were so busy testifying and catching bad guys, you forgot about the dance, and when you had the chance to ask me, you didn't have the nerve because you didn't want me to know you had forgotten it until the last minute." Kate said, laughing.

This time Steve blushed, "Now, who told you that?"

Kate laughed, "Andrew. He didn't want me to feel left out and downcast about not having a date."

"That guy is so going to get it."

She just laughed.

* * *

Kate stared at herself in the mirror.

"Come on, Kate, you look fine. Steve will be speechless when he sees you." Miley assured her friend confidently. Kate was getting ready for her date with Steve; whereas Miley was getting ready for her date with Cori. This would be Kate's first date with Steve where they would be alone, just the two of them, and maybe her last.

"Its not that. Its just that I can't believe we're leaving tomorrow." Kate answered regretfully.

"I know. It's almost unbelievable this school year is already over. It seems like just yesterday that we came here for the first time and didn't know anybody here." Miley sighed. "But oh, well. We'll be back."

"Yeah, but right now two months seems like a long way off." Kate moaned.

"I know, but we'll survive. After all, we've got each other." Miley gave Kate a hug.

Kate smiled, "Yeah, that's true. Now we better hurry, those guys will be pounding down the door in no time so we better get ready."

Miley smiled. "Right."

The girls were barely ready when Steve and Cori knocked on the door. Steve planned to take Kate to dinner and during dinner they would decide what to do afterwards.

This time both girls hurried to open the door. Steve smiled when he saw her. "Hi, you ready to go?"

Kate nodded. Bidding farewell to their friends, the two set off somewhat shyly, Kate especially. But after a while, their shyness evaporated and they talked like old friends. Therefore they had a lovely dinner. After dinner, they decided to go for a long walk in the park. They walked a distance in silence. Both had a lot to think about. Now that school was out for the summer, they would both be going their separate ways. Kate would be going back home, but she planned on coming back next fall. Steve was being transferred to another town in a few days to help with a case. He had no idea how long he'd be gone.

They had come to a stop on the bridge overlooking a sparkling, shallow river. They stood on the side of the bridge watching the water in the gathering dusk. Kate loved the river. Not only because the water was so clear, and it only being 'bout waist deep (Kate was terrified of deep, dark rivers and lakes), but because it looked so peaceful and calm. The water swirled and danced along slowly. It looked cheerful, without a care in the world. In the past year, Kate had often come to the river to think.

"So what are your plans for the summer?" Steve asked.

"I don't know. I haven't thought much about that, but I'll probably get a job or something." Kate really hadn't thought much about it. But she sure knew she was really going to miss this place.

"Well, you'll finally be rid of all us cops, huh?" Steve decided to lighten the mood a bit, things were just to serious for him on a night like this.

Kate laughed softly, "Yeah, that I will." Then she became thoughtful again. "But I'll also be rid of a couple of very good friends."

Steve smiled at her, "We'll all miss you greatly. Even my boss said he'd be sorry to see you go."

"What?! You're kidding, right? I mean, all I did was make a whole bunch of trouble for him." Kate was amazed.

"Yeah, well, I guess he doesn't mind having another pretty face around either." Steve grinned.

She burst out laughing, "No way, what's his real reason for missing me? It's got to be something other than that."

"Well, ok. He kind of liked watching me make a fool of myself whenever you were around." Steve grinned.

"Wait, you made a fool of yourself? I always thought you were a perfectionist." Kate enjoyed seeing Steve embarrassed, since it didn't happen very often, she took full advantage of it when it did.

"O come on. Knock it off." Steve pretended to be upset, but he wasn't very good at it.

"Ok, anyway, you looking forward to your new job?"

"Well, I'm kind of excited, kind of nervous, and part of me wishes I never got the job."

"Why's that?"

"I'm excited, because I always love a challenge. I'm nervous, because I don't know anyone there, and everything will be very different. And the reason I wouldn't mind if I had never gotten the job is because I'm going to miss everyone here and I don't want to leave all this behind. I love my job here. And another thing, I might not be able to be here to welcome you back this fall. I hear its supposed to be a big celebration."

Kate smiled, "I know how you feel. We'll just hope that you catch these bad guys quickly so that you can come back."

She stepped closer to him and gave him a kiss, which caught him by surprise. But recovering himself quickly, he wrapped his arms around her and kissed her back. Needless to say, they had a wonderful evening together.

* * *

That night, laying in bed, Kate smiled contentedly. She knew that everything would turn out all right. She also knew that she had made many wonderful friends in the past year, and as long as they were here, she would always be welcome. And, no matter what it took, she'd be back, in about 2 months, this fall.

She had also learned many valuable lessons in the past year. She now had more patients with others then all three of her hometown friends put together. She learned that thinking before acting really did pay off. And she learned to put a little faith in her friends, as well as strangers, again. After all, everyone is innocent until proven guilty, right? And she had learned to be her usual joyful self again, much to her friends' relief.

She could hardly wait to come back next fall.

THE END